I thought perhaps I knew things.
. . . You don't choose love.
Love chooses you.

". . . Selarom builds solid protagonists
and memorable enemies."
~*The BookLife Prize*

"Selarom has created a unique world
and culture for its inhabitants. His Jode
trilogy is a breath of fresh air in a genre
that was becoming a little stale. . ."
~ *Entrada*

PJSELAROM.COM

Available on Kindle, Amazon.com, and in other retail outlets.

All characters are fictional unless otherwise seen in a hallucination. The creatures (e.g., unipegon, asegafians, archeornyx, kiradoura, tridras, ditchightl, Dicen, etc.) are the author's proprietary property.

Dark Fantasy/Sci-fi Adventure. Mystery. Romance. Horror.

First Edition

THE JODE: Part 3: Ygl & the Dwarf

ISBN-13: 978-1-7340860-2-7 (PJ Selarom)

ISBN-10: 1-7340860-2-5

Printed in the USA. Layout by PJ Selarom.

Special thanks to the illustrators:

Corey McNaught (Map), MiblArt (Cover)

PJ SELAROM

YGL
& THE
DWARF
THE JODE: Part 3

Acknowledgments

I want to thank the love of my life, "Brit"; you're always on my mind.

My Jode Seekers, your support of and belief in this crazy series leave me no room for words. Especially Sea Breeze, who surprises me most of all.

Thanks, Charles Hubbell, for narrating the first two books.

Swen's Riddle

Across the sea of sand,
In a hidden green,
Lies the powerful Jode
Of unusual entity.

Power to rule a world.
Maybe even more.
Thou may possess it
If thee only cross the shore.

Some seek it for strength
To do what they think is right.
No matter the possessor
Many will feel its might.

Seek the danger
And Savior of the land;
Reveal the secret
Of the treachery of Man.

Main Characters

Forest of Lorel (Elves)
***Ygl**: (Pronounced EAGLE) General.
*Steadfast: Ygl's unipegon, mount.
*Welbern/Demonslayer: (WEL′ BURN) Ygl's broadsword.
***Limbus**: (LIM-BAHS′) Ygl's son.
***Ploone**: (PLOON) Limbus's best friend.
*Snip and Winky: the boys' respective asegafian cats.

Forest of Khun (Elves, Sprites, Gnomes)
***Blasmle**: (BLAS′ MAL) male Elvin chief.
*Rushar: (RU-SHAR′) Blasmle's hippogriff.
***Rungna (-Olivia)**: (RUNG′ NAH) female Elvin chief.
*Folcen'na: Rungna's hippogriff.
***Oreol**: (O-REE′ OL) Sprite chief.
***Lojstania**: (LOJ-STA′ NEE-AH) Oreol's wife.
***Mitral**: (MI′ TRAL) Gnome chief.
*Jinx: Mitral's archeornyx.
***Systoli**: (SIS-TO′ LEE) Mitral's husband.
*Rube: (ROOB) Systoli's golden cardinal.

Quirmean Empire (Man)
***Rondo**: (RON′ DO) Emperor.
***Werkle**: (WER-KLE′) Rondo's brother; advisor.
***Spenz**: (SPENZ) Rondo's youngest brother; general.
***Aman**: (EY′ MAN) Shop owner.
***Jonas**: (JO′ NAS) Princess.
***E'alor**: (EE′ A-LOR) Jonas's friend.

Giantic Estate
***Kute**: (CUTE) Prince.
*Stonecrusher: Kute's gray pegasus.
*Crater: (CRAY′ TER) Kute's large horse.
***Juna**: (JOO′ NA) Fairy queen.

*Erosc: (AY-ROSC') King, Kute's father.
*Shadocoat: (SHA-DOH' COT) Erosc's sable pegasus.
*Fabia: (FA-BEE' AH) Queen; Kute's mother.
*Kor'al: Fabia's yellow pegasus.
*Umbala: (UM' BA-LAH) Kute's brother; general.
*Slab: Umbala's red pegasus.
*Dionjor: (DEE-OWN' JOR) Erosc's brother; advisor.
*Caldera: (CAL-DARE' AH) Dionjor's emerald pegasus.
*Ood: Fairy king; Juna's husband.
*Alduur: (AL-DOOR') Shield bearer.
*Powder: Alduur's white pegasus.

Ogrean Estate
*Gravelp: (GRA' VELP) Princess.
*Hogar's Beard: (HOE' GAR) Gravelp's kiradoura.
*Smush: (SMOOSH) King.
*Dune: Smush's gryphon.
*Squash: Queen.
*Crumb: Smush's eldest son; advisor.
*Patch: Crumb's kiradoura.
*Squish: Crumb's wife.
*Punok: (PEW' NAWK) Smush's son; general.
*Pillager: Punok's gryphon.
*Gasma: Pixy queen; First Lady.
*Guisarrio: (GWEE-SAR' REE-OH) Pixy king; First Lord.
*Lady Hoodia: (HOO-DEE' AH) Pixy.
*Lord Vicstusi: (VICS-TU' SI) Hoodia's boyfriend.
*Lady Starrm: Pixy.
*Lord Zeph: (ZEF) Pixy.

Dwarven Estate
*__Qualt__: (KWALT) King.
*Bantam: Qualt's tole.
*Icon: Qualt's wolf.
*__Patina__: (PUH-TEE′ NA) Princess.
*Twilight: Patina's tole.
*Equinox: Patina's wolf.
*__Ding__: Thief.
*Red Fang: Ding's wolf.
*Gore: Ding's diamond-headed axe.

Nixy Estates
*__Sama__: (SAH′ MA) Nixy mother.
*__Ryl__: (RIL) Sama's son.
*__Isoris__: (I′ SO-RIS) Queen.
*__Tatenu__: (TA′ TEH-NOO) Isoris's sister; advisor.
*__Rahor__: (RA-WHORE′) Tatenu's brother; general.
*__Hapinset__: (HAP′ IN-SET) Tatenu's youngest brother; prince.

Miscellaneous
*Xurchon: (ZUR-CON') God of Evil.
*Tungloc: (TUNG-LOK′).
*Dicen: (DIE′ SEN).
*Tridra: (TRI′ DRA).
*Ditchightl: (DIT-CHIE′ TAL).
*Uryid: (YOU′ REE-ID).
*Los (LOSS) and Num (NUMB): Twin suns.
*Nus (NUS) and Anul (AH-NOOL′): Twin moons.
*Truba: (TROO′ BAH).
*Phorn: (FORN).
*Sreggats: (S-REH′ GAHTS).
*Cindiru: (SIN′ DIH-ROO).
*Raaligor: (RAH′ LIH-GORE).
*Kampy: (CAM′ PEE) the Decrepit.

*Elico: (EH′ LI-COH) the Huge.
*Mersa: (MER′ SAH) the Merciless.
*Dendruid: (DEHN′ DROO-ID).
*Hydroyid: (HI-DROH′ YID).
*Humad: (EW-MAD′).
*Aether: (EY′ THER).

The Divinity

Elf:
Achal: (AY′ CHAL) Lorellian goddess of memory and history; wielder of the psionic sword.
Miredo: (MEER-EH-DOH′) Khunian god of nature; wielder of the bow of storms.

Man:
Istratos: (EYE-STRA′ TOES) God of magic and games; wielder of the staff of power.
Welna: (WEL′ NAH) Goddess of the arts, wielder of the shield of creation.

Nixy:
Jeble: (JEH′ BULL) God of the sea and logic; wielder of the trident of waves.
Numr'c: (NUMB-RIC′) Goddess of dreams, fertility, and peace; embodiment of the island.

Giant:
Lolung-Cor: (LOH-LUNG′ CORE) God of war; wielder of the lance of strength.
Pyty: (PIE-TEE) Goddess of the grain; embodiment of the mountain; wielder of the sickle of sustenance.

Ogre:

Falvanch: (FAL-VANCH') Goddess of the earth; the Great Sculptor; wielder of the club of order.

Hogar: (HOE' GAR) God of resilience; embodiment of the desert; the Rock Shaker; wielder of the pick of chaos.

Dwarf:

Henc: (HENC) God of wealth; wielder of the axe of winter.

Pariot: (PEY-REE' AWT) Goddess of invention; wielder of the hammer of sacred magma.

Faerie (Fairies, Pixies, Sprites; Gnomes):

Ethnel: (ETH' NEL) Essence of preservation and small creatures; wielder of the dagger of luck.

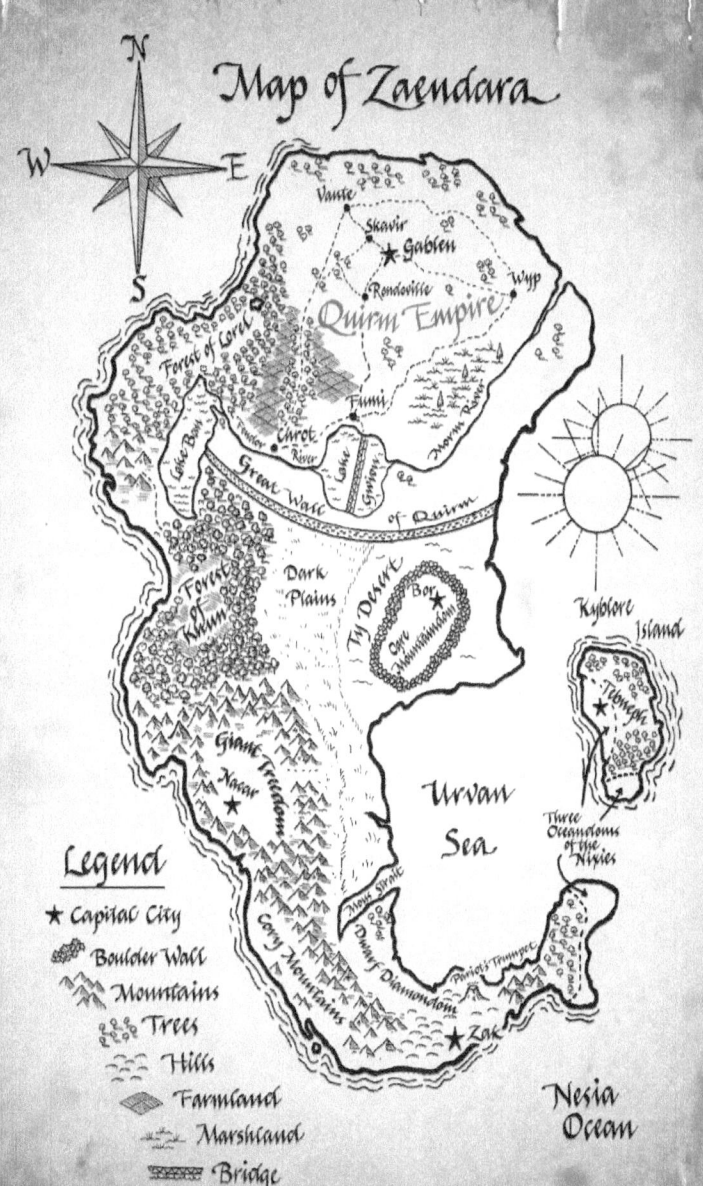

PROLOGUE: Queen Squash

Salutations.
I am Achal, Lorellian goddess of
memory and history.
Welcome back to Inner Earth in crisis. I will
continue to narrate while General Ygl
narrates his parts.

The Ogrean Queen clambered to her bedroom's vaulted window, wrapped in her furry blankets, awakened by and engulfed in a new feeling she could not comprehend.

Darkness's silence soothed cool and deafening from the night. The air, just too frigid in the Grand Spire. Her breath almost curled before her like a wispy fog created by King Zeph or Queen Hoodia of the Pixy Council. The council members' divine right was limited to making gases, much like her gift granted by the Divinity.

"Oh, Smush," Squash mumbled. She could not sleep upon her bed of gravel.

Several nights had passed since King Smush left Bor, the Ogrean estate's capital. Squash was not used to being unaccompanied by her husband. Their sons and he had marshaled a huge army to war against the Giants as a preventive measure, leaving her to rule in his absence.

Crumb, her eldest son, must have been right about Gravelp, her eldest daughter, being a traitor. How could Gravelp turn against her own people?

Murder Crumb's wife? In favor of that "Party of the Jode"?

Unusual, Squash thought. As she crossed the marble flooring, she listened for the desert cockatrice's *hoo-hoo* or the Ty toad's ratcheted croaking she had grown so accustomed to throughout her life.

She could hear none.

She rubbed her hand against the window's red alabaster sill while scanning the domed rooftops to the desert region's sands beyond her stony kingdom's walls, calling upon her divine right to change earthen substances. The red alabaster transformed into lavender porcelain from the rubbing's origin, lustrous in the shiny wave.

The ebony queen almost chuckled to herself. Smush would never attempt such a feat. Creating such pretty colors and materials was never his interest—shaping rock, another matter. Her divine right, hers and hers alone. Like any queen.

Almost as powerful as her husband, Squash felt she governed the kingdom with capable hands, though she did not know how capable her hands would be. When King Smush held steady rule, she would sightsee, making cavernous structures prettier and, on occasion, functional.

And the dream that pulled her from sleep? Her dream, she realized, was a memory—a returning forgotten memory revealing she was never royalty. Just a common citizen.

Why? How could she forget something so important? Her being so common, like the public her family adored?

Why did she forget?

In this memory, she met then-Prince Smush while teaching on an educational trip she spearheaded, and her life changed. How could she forget their awkward lingering glances at each other? His modesty? She had made it a point to complete her schooling before getting too involved with her now-husband. Nonetheless, love played its silly game, and the Divinity favored her much. Teaching still simmered in her blood, though as queen, she deemed she had much to learn.

Was Smush right to leave her alone to rule? A former teacher? Was his decision responsible? Could their smart son, Crumb, not have stayed behind? Someone from the Pixy Council should have stayed with her.

Traitorous Gravelp fled with the foreign troublemakers—Ygl, Kute, and Ding of the Party of the Jode—after Squish's murder in the palace. Queen Squash felt sorry for Crumb, for Squish had been his wife.

The queen leaned her rotund belly against the window's arch, upset by her daughter's treachery, fiddling with her ivory earrings, appreciating the cityscape.

Night's blackness could have overwhelmed her kingdom for years to come if the citizens had not created these streetlamp posts along the cobblestone roadways with her husband's guidance. Of course, she had created the posts' orbs that soaked and reflected the twin suns' rays, basking the estate in a soft luminance during the twin moons' passage, guiding citizens home. The task proved quite challenging, yet the queen would do anything to please her estate, her public.

The lampposts' luminance extended toward the Ty Desert, beyond looming crude walls that discouraged unwelcome visitors. The luminance's fading edges played with the night sky's fringes.

Squash noticed the pleasant flirtation was different this evening, for the sky seemed to encroach upon the fringe—undermining it.

A milky mist with bluish-yellow sparkles slipped across the outer sands, startling the queen. "Oh my. This mist Gravelp try tell Smush and me about? Oh my," she noted in her race's broken language.

A scream in the streets in front of the palace. A tall, slithering creature chased a citizen down the cobblestone roads. They were hard to distinguish from her vantage point up high, as the two figures only reappeared where the lamps' lights permitted. The startled queen noticed the creature's clicking, elongated claws stabbed into the roadway along their path.

No, not claws. Fangs. Fangs spewing acidic venom with each clash.

Was this the creature Gravelp had warned the family about? The monster that killed the orphans? Had Gravelp not killed the orphans?

With a quick wave of her hand, Squash cast her divine right as best she could past the pious statues fencing her palace, past the nobilities' village, past the promenade to the palace lined with thirty-foot spires coated with lustrous stones, and past the promenade's granite archway.

Her divine right touched the stony space between hunter and prey, absorbing into the cobblestone, altering its hardened masterpiece into talcum dust, causing the surprised monster to fall into a makeshift pit, then transforming the pit and dust into thickened granite, sealing the monster's fate.

What had just happened? No one expected these phenomena to occur. Yes, she knew of the attacks within her estate, but the scoundrels had never appeared so brazen.

Squash had thought reigning in Smush's absence would be easy. What was she to do now? She ran across her bedroom chambers and slid open the marble door. Her breath almost caught up with her racing heart.

"Yes, Queen?" an alarmed guard asked, clubbed mace at hand. He puzzled both of them with his change in dialect. He should have called her "Hill."

"Get guards to kingdom's borders." She deflected her worry about a dialect change she had no choice but to embrace. "Order citizens seal all entrances to homes." She sprinted down the halls, wrapped in her blankets.

"Where you going?" her sentry asked.

"Me go get daughter." Daughter? She should have said "pebble." Kingdom? She should have said "mountaindom."

Squash balked in her rush, remembering the odd feeling that had awoken her, realizing the effect: her dialect had indeed disappeared. She found her people and herself speaking like her smart son, Advisor Crumb.

Like Man.

Chapter 1: Leaves

Gablen, Quirm's capital

Man's empire

The Elvin servant stepped away after providing Emperor Rondo and his blonde consort their breakfast.

Rondo took a bite of his poached egg, the peppery bolus sliding down his throat. *The moment is almost upon us,* he thought while chewing on another morsel. His cup of almond tea still brewed hot to his right, balancing his Demonguards' trace stenches. He'd ordered most of the Demonguards out of the dining room and into the hallway, but the smells lingered. How Xurchon could even bear the unnatural stench was beyond the embattled emperor.

Another sunny late morning—the twin suns peaked in a cloudless firmament. Rondo could see his sprawling city's stony ramparts from his balcony's dining area, glad that the surge in rebellions had somehow come to a halt. Possibly.

"Why do these people not love me?" he mumbled, fretting about his enemies. "Can they not see my conquest is for their own good? We ruled Zaendara before, and this was tranquil." He took a sip; the almond tea's honey coated the egg's spicy aftertaste.

"Rondo." Xurchon's vacant voice startled Rondo's mind.

The emperor's sullen eyes shifted left, then right, searching for his chosen god. "Where are you?"

"I'm here."

Rondo looked again, even around his chair. "Where?"

"Here. Below thee."

Rondo looked into his teacup. His god's youthful visage floated in the reflection; his hair's curls thrashed about like cream. "Mighty Xurchon, can I not have a little bit of privacy?"

"I see everything."

"And what have you seen today?"

"The mist. Thou hesitates to send it in."

"Do you think now is appropriate? My brother, General Spenz, isn't here to advise me. He's in the Dwarf kingdom playing his flute to keep order." The emperor pursed his lips. "Why can't you send your Demons?"

"Thou knows, Rondo, my children rely upon thy jodepiece's mist to breach the wall between our worlds. Few of my children can enter thy world, but that depends upon how much stronger my influence is."

Rondo tried not looking at the murky liquid. "Demonsia."

"Yes, demonsia. The ability of my children to not only possess a mortal but transform the mortal into them, but that works only if the mortal accepts my mark upon them. Thy Demonguards and the Dicen ravaging the Ogrean estate are fine examples.

"Magic is thy family's divine right, but thou knows how limited it is, needing a means for its use— like Spenz needing a musical instrument to focus his. The jodepiece is powerful enough to boost thy gift, giving a taste of what it's like to go beyond being

hindered by the need of a medium. Even with the need for a medium, Man's divine right towers over the other races, for their gifts are conclusive while thine expands. Once we procure the entire Jode, thy influence will go beyond thy imagination."

"I will rule Zaendara's nations."

"Not just that, but all Inner Earth."

Man's emperor balked. He hadn't thought about that, protecting his thoughts from his new god.

Xurchon continued, his eyelids in the cream creased with pleasure. *"Don't lose faith, Rondo. All things shall come when due. The Ogres' forces are upon the Giants' estate, and thy mist simply waits. Thou must strike before the Ogrean queen builds up more defenses."*

"What is she doing?" Rondo perked up, taking another bite of egg.

"She's entombed her royal subjects and herself within her palace. With her divine right, she has transformed her palace window panels into shifting marble to seal her windows to withstand the mist. She's also instructed her people to barricade themselves within their homes. Her guards—"

"Why not let them suffocate themselves, mighty Xurchon?" The emperor shifted his disapproving gaze. He wondered if he drank the tea, maybe Xurchon would go away.

The tea's cream curved into a smile. *"That's a novel idea, but why wait so long, Rondo? I did not know patience was a virtue of thine."*

Patience was a price Rondo could do without.

"Don't worry, Rondo. My strongest children, the Truba, are slowly breaching the wall between our worlds. They don't need my marking on anyone to perform that act. Some of them, the Raaligor, are

already doing that. My Raaligor will set things right in Quirm."

"Your Raaligor?"

"They'll hunt to keep things in order. Kampy the Decrepit, Elico the Huge, and Mersa the Merciless. They are of shadow. Shadow of them." Xurchon vanished into the almond swirls.

The emperor grimaced at the statement. He motioned the Elvin servant to replace the almond tea with a new cup.

His blonde consort refused to touch her ham omelet, a slight slant to her eyes. "Your magic made me look like you," she stated with surprise, her curiosity equal to her beauty.

"I have Vantenian in my heritage. You come across smart like one. Insightful. It's important for me to disguise your scaly skin to make you more presentable to my court. You've been in my bedchambers so long."

"Are you all right?" Seeing him speak to tea baffled the camouflaged Nixy a bit.

"I'm fine."

She surveyed his opulent dining chamber, minus his bedroom's pelts. Fleecy carpeting from Wyp spread beneath them in a sea of green decked with platinum netting. Fine-dining ware from Skavir filled shapely oaken cabinets from the same city. "Continue the castle tour after we eat?"

"Of course. Sama?"

The male servant provided him a new cup and left.

"Yes, Emperor?"

"It doesn't bother you that you're speaking like me? Your dialect gone? Your descriptive flips gone?" Rondo took a satisfying sip.

Sama smiled with shy eyes. "No. Not at all. I mean, it's a bit weird, but it's better for us to understand each other."

He nodded at the potted ivy behind her upon a pedestal. "I don't know why you brought that. You take it everywhere. You should've left it in the bedchamber."

"It reminds me of my son, Ryl."

Rondo knew the Nixy mother trusted him, unaware of how much more warden he was to her than savior. This emperor who took her away from Ryl with a murderous Death Mist that conquered the Forest of Lorel. A mist that conquered the Dwarven estate. Her Ryl, his hair a mesh of vines.

"Your son?" Rondo's interest was piqued. These couple of months she'd been his prisoner, she'd never raised the notion.

"Yes. He's missing. Could you help me find him?"

"I don't know."

"You could help. You could help me know who I am. Where he is. I know—" Sama leaned forward.

"Shh." Rondo didn't want her to let Xurchon know his little secret—his jodepiece dangling from his neck granted him telepathy. This crystal artifact, assumed to wield only magic, wielded a power Xurchon refused to reveal to faithful Rondo, a divine right belonging only to Ygl and Methelo of the Lorellian Elves.

He downed the rest of his almond tea to avert any more unwanted godly entrances.

Rondo found himself distrusting his new god. Regret, a sour pill. Why didn't Xurchon tell him the jodepiece had psionic properties? "I could try to help,

Sama. You, of course, helped me out. I can only return the favor. Do you know the father?"

"No." Sama leaned back, feeling the lacy tablecloth upon the round table. "Emperor, when we walked through your throne room . . . those empty thrones. Do you have children? Did you have a wife?"

He tried not to think of them, his children—his failures. His wife needed vengeance. If his leadership thrived in a foul world, let justice be done. "Yes, I had three children. Two girls and a boy."

"The three thrones facing yours from your dais?"

"Yes."

"Your wife?"

"Her name was Maxis. A powerful female who could never be satisfied."

"How could she not be satisfied with you? You saved me from that mist. You're a good person."

A good person? Rondo grimaced at his tall prisoner's compliment. She and her missing son were just in the way of the Forest of Lorel's conquest. With his newfound psionics, he erased his past truth from her mind. She must never remember that he'd killed and maimed in the name of love. She should never know the truth that a war waged outside his capital. A war he would soon win and, with that, all of Zaendara's heart.

And his loving citizens should never know he consorted with the enemy.

With mighty Xurchon's help, he would soon have the Jode. "You haven't eaten your omelet."

"I'm . . . I'm not used to this. I don't know what it is."

"Maybe something better." With his index finger's slight gesture, bluish-yellow spangles floated to her breakfast, transforming the protein-rich meal into something alike, full of protein, a raw halibut garlanded with small tomatoes and lettuce.

Surprised, Sama's fingers touched her smiling mouth. "You. You're too kind, Emperor."

Rondo figured she remembered how he'd changed his bedroom into her private resort, furnished with an extravagant lagoon.

"Where there's a mirror . . ." He repeated part of her advice to him weeks ago. With another slight gesture, his bluish-yellow spangles peeled some of her face's illusion, revealing bluish-green scales. He found himself falling for this exotic Elf dealing with amnesia.

"There's love?" Sama queried.

The Elvin servant observed the back of Rondo's head from the doorway, amazed that the woman the Quirmean consorted with was a Demon. That female must be a Demon. No Elf looked like that. Lorellian or Khunian.

He pulled at the butter knife hidden in his sleeve. He would serve Captain Lyp and the rebellion well, killing this emperor for all Lorel. The opportunity was nigh with so few Demonguards in the dining room.

A giggle from down the hallway.

Odd. A Lorellian boy skipped past the male servant, poking the servant's side twice with a pair of dirty fingers.

Nervous and shocked, the servant pursued the Elvin boy, knowing children shouldn't be on this side of the castle, especially Elvin ones.

The boy skipped into a dim pantry where the servant had prepared the received meals. The servant tried looking for the boy but couldn't find him. Sensing an increase in warmth, the servant turned to the creaking door behind him. The giggling boy stood behind the closing door.

Odd . . . half the boy seemed to melt into the growing shadows, his giggle evolving into a cackling hiss.

The room felt warmer. This was no Lorellian boy.

"Wh-what are you?" the nervous servant inquired.

The boy's fingers pressed against his half lips as he cackled a giggle. His dirty fingers pointed to the servant's side, soaked wet with blood where the boy had poked him.

The shocked Lorellian pulled out his butter knife. His initial shock wasn't because of the errant boy but because of a poking stab.

"How? Get away from me, monster."

With barely any light in the room, except for a few candles, the boy was absorbed into the umbra, becoming shadow. His spirited Elvin eyes reverted to a vacuous gray that lowered as protrusions jutted from the hunching creature's elbows.

The frightened servant swiped and swiped at the hissing umbra scuttling closer to him.

The room felt hotter and hotter.

The creature hissed another cackle. "You belong to Kampy the Decrepit of the Raaligor, mortal. Xurchon would be happy. I'm ahead of you, Elico and Mersa."

The Demonguards, hearing the servant's scream, didn't budge from their hallway posts.

Chapter 2: Steadfast

My pegasus, Claybreaker, trailed behind Ding's rusty-gray pegasus, Slateripper, as they swerved to the right over the Urvan Sea, Claybreaker's indigo wings heaving.

We journeyed all night over the glittering terrain—an interesting affair as we headed toward Kyblore Island, seeking the inhabitants' assistance against Man and Xurchon's psychotic plan to rule with the powerful Jode. A plan we dared not see to fruition if our estranged estates were to remain in peace and harmony.

The twin suns' afternoon shine proved an inviting ally to the salty sea air, aside from nervous Ding's unavoidable antics on his unrelenting mount's spine.

Funny. What happened to my dialect? I should have said "m-moonday," not night. "Afternoon" was definitely Quirmean.

Swen's riddle still rattled me. Twice, I thought the "hidden green" was in the Ogrean estate and that Xurchon had tricked us when I thought it was in Crumb's malachite home and in the hourglass that imprisoned Juna. This Jode must be found with its "power to rule the world." Of course, I knew this power as I struggled with the "unusual entity" in my jodepiece I wore as a charm around my neck whose powerful magicks had saved me more than once against Rondo's piece, the Death Mist, and even Xurchon.

Swen, my genie . . .

Ygl & the Dwarf

How relaxing. The algae beds' lush, green meadows dispersed into the horizon. Ding and I needed the leisure, considering I had to deal with the Dicen's wound to my right gut. A Dicen, appearing like Crumb's dead wife, Squish, had attacked me before we left the Giantic estate. Princess Gravelp luckily arrived, casting Dicen Squish into the Mous Strait with her divine right to shatter earth.

The night's better part was spent dealing with my healing process through my challenging jodepiece, which did not make things easy for me, making me grateful for Swen's mystic coddling hiding us from Xurchon. But my alluring genie could only help so much, leaving me to perform the healing—and still wonder about her, my attraction growing for her, superseding what I felt for Giantic Kute and my deceased Thalla, my wife.

A very delicate process. I remained wary of my piece's sentient being as I proceeded with mending my torn flesh. The wound, not that deep. No need to rush these things, considering the sentient being's knack for trying to control me.

I hoped the rest of the Party of the Jode fared better. However, with half my humanity floating within my piece's matrix, soaking in mystic energy shared by them with Swen's help, the Party and I were better off with my jodepiece's protection against Xurchon and Emperor Rondo.

Fish I had never seen before swam below, near the water's surface, in big groups. A strange abundance. Ding stated the groups were called "schools," which he believed the Nixies called their people. Fish at Lorel appeared boring, with their similar grayish scales and small bodies, compared to these flashy fish that seemed to take the Urvan's glittery waves with them when some of them popped out during a swim.

So many. Were the fish interested in us? Many swam below the waves. And how interesting to note our races named certain facets of our culture after that which had the most influence. Did it matter now? Many of our dialects had disappeared.

"And what do you call your kin, Ding?" I performed my best effort to keep up with his awkward flight pattern. He fumbled so much on Slateripper's spine that he kept pulling on the reins, confusing the pegasus, making his mount swerve in different directions. I hoped we traveled in the correct one.

"My 'kin,' Elf," he answered impatiently, "would have been called a 'people.'"

"People?"

Ding flinched at the dialect change as well, as I noticed a bit of mine still available. "Oh, Elf! Can you not wait?" His fumbled words tumbled out as he attempted to change the subject. I tried retaining a laugh.

I could not blame Ding for his turmoil, for him being an individual thriving so close to land. For a moment, I had that luxury in my life when I was a child who owned an asegafian cat. As it became apparent I could no longer ride a wild pet, Scall, my dad, presented me with a special gift at sixteen years of age—my favorite steed, Steadfast, my unipegon. I could never ride my asegafian again because he met his death when I was a child, and the blame became mine when my cat came to the defense of my mom, Rarle, against the Dicen who killed her.

Steadfast became my asegafian's honorable replacement years later, presented to me from the Forest of Khun in part because of my grief over losing my mom. As a newfound general trained by Khunian Elves, I had already shown Scall I could lead Lorellians as well as he did. It was prudent to pass the proverbial scroll. Scrolls, the mantles of power where we wrote our history.

Steadfast and I had known each other since my Khunian training. However, this meeting proved an awkward moment for both of us. I stood transfixed before what all Lorel considered the most beautiful, ravishing creature in Zaendara.

I felt I did not deserve my unipegon, and he was not ready for the transfer to me. I remembered staring into his reptilian eyes, noble orbs, whispering telepathically to him. *"I do not own the gift of ani-speak granted by great Miredo to Rungna-Olivia of Khun. It is important for me to tell you I will be as much your psyche as you are my soul, and I will be as much your soul as you are my psyche. Please do not be offended."*

Miredo, the god of nature and life, was my goddess Achal's lover but not my deity. His divine right was never granted upon my royalty. Hence, Achal granted our psionic gifts. I would have been grateful to own Miredo's gifts so that I could understand Steadfast better.

Even so, the dilemma seemed not to matter. I admired my unipegon's angular face, a face appearing much like a unicorn's, yet its frame stolen from a dragon, as if the opposing beasts may have mated in an unholy union.

Yet something told me Steadfast had attained the purest spirit. Wild but pure. I just knew he seemed separate from other beasts. For him to have never known love for another of his breed must have been devastating, and so Lorellians became his mate and showed him much respect. As general, I gave

Steadfast as much love as I did my wife, Thalla—maybe even more.

My brother, Methelo, of course, fretted a bit but later accepted Steadfast as a better match for me and not him. He accepted my understanding of Steadfast's solitude as he studied under our father's wing, and I maintained the mantle of Lorel's first general, primed and ready to lead our army. I taught our reluctant kin everything I knew; however, I did not feel as fulfilled as I had thought I would.

My loneliness would seem endless despite Thalla's fondness until I stared into Steadfast's opulent eyes. I did not need any gifts to understand how forlorn my unipegon felt as well. To this effect, my unique mount and I felt like brothers. I knew what his every snort meant, and when a significant one arose, my forehead would snuggle against his, my fingers scratching his mandible. Solitude became a true tie that could bind.

The ride's joy was another feeling my mount and I shared. The freedom to rise higher into the sky than any hippogriff, a thrill most exhilarating. The thought of someday reaching the heavens and visiting the Divinity spelled a challenge worth taking. A challenge Steadfast refused. Nonetheless, the ride became an escapist's blessing.

"Damn, Elf," Ding exclaimed. "Have we reached the outer sky already?"

Ding's outcry and a sea of clouds broke me from my rambling revelry. *Did he read my mind?* A telepathic recheck made sure I severed our link. "No, Ding. It appears the outer sky has met us." Indeed, a light fog had swept in from fifty feet above. "The question, my friend, is 'Are we at our destination?'"

I scanned behind me. No land could be perceived along the Urvan Sea's glittery width.

Higher above, a storm cloud poked out a bumpy head in the fog's front, racing it.

Ding snorted. "Kyblore Island is not too far away. Believe me, there is no one who wants to get there quicker than me."

Chapter 3: Limbus, Ygl's Son, the "Little General"

Outside the Forest of Lorel.
Afternoon.

"Bloodfather! Dad!" Limbus yelled, awakening from his slumber upon the grasses, Los and Num's sunny glare blinding his pupils.

"Limbus." Ploone, Limbus's best friend, hurried to his aid, touching Limbus's shoulder along the mountainside facing the Forest of Lorel a mile away. "L, are you OK?"

Their resting asegafian cats, Snip and Winky, jumped from the excitement, mauve eyes blinking. Their mounts would never leave the boys' side.

"I miss my dad." Limbus wept, holding Ploone tightly. They sat near the path facing Lorel. Best friends since birth. Fourteen years.

From its perch thirty miles away, a triangular establishment of three sequoias poked above the arboreal landscape, bearing three tiers of his family's home, the Majestic Treehouse. The final tenement, the royal chambers, rested atop, almost three hundred feet from the ground. His mother, Thalla, had helped build the treehouse.

"I miss my parents too," hefty Ploone replied with quiet concern.

A scattering of leaves cycled through the air from Lorel in their direction.

Ygl & the Dwarf

"It has been a couple of days since we started talking Quirmean. There must be meaning behind this." Limbus fretted about the absurd dialect change.

"Yes, it has been a couple of days. We should be attacking them for taking our home," Ploone insisted. His thick fingers adjusted his Khunian helmet. He waved a fist at their hidden adversary within Lorel's light-green canopies.

"We are not ready," Limbus argued, staring at the grass. He looked back at Ploone, appreciating his determined friend. "I had another dream again—more like a memory, like what my dad has."

"A memorial dream, huh? Like when Swen showed the Protectors when we were attacked by that mist?" Ploone stood, determined, placing his hands on his hips, facing their adversary.

"Maybe. It seemed so real, like it happened just last year. I was being chased by a Fumian wearing a crown, I think. She was very intimidating. And I was running with an older girl down a cobblestone path, and my shoulder struck a castle wall's corner. The girl had white hair and was tanned like us—"

"A Lorellian?"

"No! She was dressed really nice. A princess, maybe. We were both running from the Fumian."

The cycling leaves floated through the friends' area.

Limbus turned, watching the asegafians' mauve eyes blinking with excitement as the felines chased the leaves, their butterfly tongues flicking with each bounce, trying to catch one.

"Yip, yip," the asegafians barked.

Limbus regarded a force field encapsulating the Khunian Protectors' sacred forest in a shimmering chlorophyllic green beyond the mountains' south rim.

Ploone was perplexed, thinking about the tanned girl with white hair. "Emperor Rondo has children?"

"I guess. Dad barely took me there."

"Well, you had a memorial dream about a castle. Sounds like you have been there a lot."

Limbus shut down for a moment. "I fear my dad is dead." He felt Ploone rubbing his head.

"If General Ygl was dead, we would have all felt it, Limbus. Come on. Stop it."

"General Ygl?" A passing racajaandoo leaf stopped in midcycle.

Surprised, Limbus yelped at the speaking leaf's query, despite brave Ploone.

The floating leaf's petiole separated into dainty legs, the slender blade into multiple wings the same color, revealing . . .

"Chieftess Lojstania of the Sprites." Limbus's eyebrows arched.

A few of the other cycling leaves returned to their Sprite forms, accompanying their chieftess.

She fluttered closer before the boys in her split dress. "Little Limbus, I thought that was you."

"Lojstania, I want to thank you for protecting Khun." Limbus gestured to the immense force field. He knew Khun was more fertile and plush than Lorel could ever be.

Lojstania blushed. "Well, it was not just me. Chief Mitral and my husband had a hand in it too."

"Oh yes. Some are calling you 'the Trinity.' Boy, Chief Mitral looks so different. Black like deep earth and all. He looks like a walking rock. How is Chief Oreol?"

Ygl & the Dwarf

"He is still sitting atop the half jodepiece Ygl left us, maintaining the barrier. It saddens me how that crystal has some sort of hold over him, but we need it."

"I agree. Can your divine right over the flowering trees help Lorel?"

She smiled. "Of course. But I must leave to update the other chiefs on what we surveilled over there."

"What did you see?"

She hesitated with a honeyed smile, smelling like fresh foliage. "Well, can you keep it between the three of us?"

"Of course," the boys chimed.

"A Quirmean royal fights against the soldiers there. A princess."

"Wow!"

"Did she have snowy hair?" Limbus asked.

"No. I am not clear what her divine right is, but she would present Blasmle and Rungna-Olivia quite a challenge if she was fighting them. Jonas is her name, I believe. I must go. Moments cannot be wasted." She fluttered away with the rest of her entourage to her needed rendezvous with the Protectors' other chiefs.

"Wow," Ploone stated. "The Quirmeans are fighting each other. Who would have known?"

Limbus looked away, sad. "I suck."

"Suck what? Water?"

"No. I am just bad at everything," Limbus insisted.

"Oh, more Quirmean lingo," Ploone realized. "L, you do not 'suck.' You saved all the Lorellian children from that mist. That was you. No one else."

"Remember four years ago when you came with Dad and me to Khun?"

PJ Selarom

"Yeah. You and I did some sword fighting."

"And you kept beating me."

"Oh, that was luck, L."

"No, it was not. You have an instinct for combat, Ploone. It flows from you," Limbus insisted.

"I guess. But do not worry. When your dad came around to check on us, I covered for you."

"Yeah, you made it look like I was beating you."

"It was great." Ploone chuckled.

"No, it was not. You should be the general, Ploone."

"What? No way. You are the leader." Ploone squatted down to Limbus. "What does Rungna call you? 'Little General?'" he teased, punching Limbus on the shoulder. He grinned, trying to tickle his friend's side.

"She calls me that because I saved her from a Quirmean arrow when her forces charged at them from western Khun. But you really have no fear." Limbus resisted getting tickled, pushing away from Ploone. "I mean, no one picks on me because I am the general's son, but you were always picked on because of your weight or how you seem a bit slower than others, and it never bothered you. You are just fearless."

Ploone paused in thought, as if absorbing the cloudless spring sky. "I do have fear."

"No, you do not, Ploone. Look how I jumped when Lojstania made herself known. You did not."

"I do, L. Just because I do not show it does not mean I do not have it. Listen, even with Quirm's attack upon Khun, you led us. I did not. You are the leader, and we are your brigade. The Children's Brigade, Limbus. Do not forget that."

Limbus shook, realizing Ploone's words spun true. He had to make his dad proud. "Blasmle and Rungna-Olivia lead all of us. We follow their orders for our next move. Achal, guide us all." He glanced at Lorel with his best friend.

One thing Limbus wished he had not followed his parents' footsteps on was not meditating. Ploone was always the calmer of the two. Some Soft Winds meditation could do the "Little General" good.

Chapter 4: Queen Fabia and the Gathering

The Cory Mountains
Giantic estate

Queen Fabia, Erosc's wife, never believed herself above helping others—just above drama. She mingled amongst her citizens, carrying parcels and wielding her sickle-lance. The lance bore streamers in the oncoming currents. Fabia knew the masses' gradual climb to worthier shelter would eventually relieve them.

Fabia's guards assisted the Giantic folks' evasion southwest past their capital, Nacar, almost hiding within the Cories' flanks from the oncoming war. Wives and mothers assisted many elders along the way. Even older children gave assistance. Many citizens carried parcels for sustenance, though not much since the southern refuge held plenty because of the feared Coming of the Unknown Land hailing destruction to Zaendara. The Coming could be fable, but Giants always liked being prepared.

Fabia rode in a dignified way, legs to her left, upon her yellow pegasus, Kor'al—so named after the Giants' respected region. She, too, wore Dwarven tungsten armor like Erosc, but only so she could see her face upon the vambrace. She had traded her manticora-skinned slippers for bronzy boots.

Who knew? After the Giants defeated the Ogrean invaders, her estate would conquer the

Ygl & the Dwarf

Ogrean estate, granting her access to their interesting garments made of . . . what was that material called? Silk?

A boyish duo sparred with long cornstalks in front of her. "Take that, you Ogre monster!" the shorter boy shouted at his taller competitor, who was wearing a stuffed potato sack. Their antics annoyed some of the evaders on behalf of the warriors who organized upon the battlefield, but Queen Fabia pursed her lips against all this "drama."

War is what we are. It is but part of the circle we grow in.

She rose above every "drama," including little children sparring with cornstalks, because she knew she was stationed closer to the Divinity than anybody, and she wanted everyone to remember that. The brats reminded her of her older children, Prince Kute and his transgender brother, General Umbala.

The brat costumed like an Ogre tripped before Fabia's mount. The rambunctious child screamed, fearing a piercing from Kor'al's sharpened horseshoes.

"Kor'al," the calm Fabia commanded.

The frightened child glanced up at the towering equine, freezing. His friend instinctively stopped in agreement.

The queen did not miss a beat, refusing to look at them. "Pick him up," she commanded the friend. Her gaze, unflinching, surveyed the passersby. Some stopped; others kept trudging. "You are not ready for battle, child, if a pair of hooves frightens you. Nonetheless, Lolung-Cor and Pyty will be proud of you someday. Try not to fall in front of Kor'al again." Her long cotton skirt draped over Kor'al's saddle, billowing. Random vines dangled from her waist.

Witnesses gaped at their queen's changed dialect. She hesitated as well—noticing she had said "someday" instead of "some cloudnoon"—but she shrugged the phenomenon off. More important matters lay at hand.

Gasps and shouts emitted twenty feet from her. A feeble old man had fallen in the crowd, overburdened with too many parcels. Some refugees went to assist him. His groan, very loud.

"Oh." Fabia sighed. "Why must there be so much commotion?" She slid off Kor'al to assist the fatigued old man.

The crowd moved aside to allow her a path. As she approached, Fabia perceived the old man as her son, Kute, lying upon the ground, wounded, a victim of the Dark Plains' creatures.

A slight gasp escaped her as she tried to shove off the image. She handed her sickle-lance to an awaiting guard and knelt to assist the senior. She had to be strong. "Come, sir."

"Oh, my queen, I am so sorry." He smelled like some of the rotting fruits and vegetables permeating the air, unlike the scented garland of tiny tomatoes her short blonde hair sported.

"You should not have taken so many belongings—"

"I know."

"You should have instead bathed."

"Yes. I am sorry."

She held the tired Giant close, sensing a slight shiver escape him. His face pressed against her breastplate's aegis that resembled a fruity cornucopia mixed with vegetables swerving down her armor's midpoint.

Ygl & the Dwarf

We believe in war, yet some shiver, she thought. *Lolung-Cor, give us strength.* She looked around as she held him. "What is your name?"

"I am too tired to remember, my queen."

"Come." She held him closer despite his stench. "Let my strength be yours." Her fingers, moistened by opava butter, touched his chest as she surrendered to her holy moment. A flow rich with natural energy streamed from within her and into the tired elder, representing her breastplate's aegis—the gift of the divine granted solely to her. The divine right of replenishment not even King Erosc could boast.

In a slow ebb, the old man felt his strength returning. The spectators clapped, awed as he stood, revitalized.

His slight nod and teary eyes expressed enough gratitude. "My queen."

Not once did Fabia look at him. It was just too much drama, but she needed to set an example. "Come, I will carry some parcels for you. You can bathe at my place when we get to safety."

That example would tell her public they had nothing to fear.

She sighed.

Overhead, a cavalry upon pegasi rode by. The wind stirred, nippy. Storm clouds approached from the east and south.

Five miles north, outside the mountains' range, Prince Kute nodded, glancing back at the Cories from the dry pasture with his army. He was satisfied the looming pile of boulders blocking the kingdom's entrances remained secured as the Ogres and Giants confronted each other with a mile's worth of land between them. He knew his mother led their people to safety somewhere south in the protected region.

Contrary to his army wanting to demolish the Ogrean invaders, Kute desired an amicable solution. He hoped Ygl and Ding fared better with the Nixies.

He was glad his brother, General Umbala, covered the skyways with an equal force built to challenge the Ogres. *Nobody could be a better general.*

Pegasi soared with their riders, sharpened hooves glistening in Los and Num's shameless sunlight; their owners flaunting sickles, lances, and sickle-lances. On the mountainside, the same weaponry sloped in somewhat greater numbers. No more did the Giants till the fields while their children played. No more did the citizenry prepare for war, for war had arrived upon the kingdom's doorstep.

Prince Kute scratched his conditioned beard. The wind aerated the tense scene with a fibrous intoxication boiling with pectin and bran. "Do you smell that?" he asked his father.

"The plantations provide much nourishment—even to our senses," smug King Erosc affirmed. The jewels on his braided beard clattered.

"I smell spoil, but you are correct, Father."

Strapping General Umbala added, "Soon the scent of blood and sweat will mix with it as well." Crimson Slab, Umbala's striped pegasus, jostled, grunting in agreement.

Erosc keeled over in pain upon his saddle, his bejeweled braids clattering. Kute remembered Advisor Crumb doing the same thing at the Ogrean estate.

"Father?" Kute and Umbala chorused with concern.

"I am . . . I am fine," Erosc retorted.

Umbala was not satisfied. "You had this same issue before Kute's homecoming. Dionjor had—"

"That was then. This is now, Sifya." Erosc emphasized Umbala's former name, his dead name, as a slur, insulting the transgender general.

Ogrean Princess Gravelp touched Umbala's hand, comforting him. Kute noticed how uncomfortable his brother was with the Ogre's presence.

"What Umbala says is true, Father," Kute added, defending his brother. "The crops are probably spoiling because of your sickness. But we will prevail."

"King Erosc." A scout landed beside the black-armored king upon a blue-violet pegasus. "In the distance, a small band approaches."

Kute peered over the tanned grasses that faded into the Dark Plains' southern outskirts, noticing the dark-skinned grouping not far away.

"They are waving a white flag," he noted.

"Surrender?" General Umbala surmised. "This is strange behavior."

Advisor Dionjor chimed in, "They have stopped midfield. It appears they want a conference, Erosc."

"What do we do, Dionjor?" Erosc asked his brother, taking a puff from his long briar pipe, enjoying the minty tobacco.

"W-we go s-speak them," Ogrean Gravelp answered in her broken language, hoping her position as a possible liaison would suffice.

For a moment, silence befell the gathering. Only pegasi flapping wings rippled with the increasing currents.

"Princess Gravelp." Erosc kept staring ahead, examining the white banner. "You are with us only because my son believes in you despite my overture to you."

"And I still do, Father." Kute defended her while adjusting his furry jacket over his bronzy breastplate. He sighed. *I wish everything would be more jovial.* It would be. "The princess has been there for me, and I shall be there for the princess. I say we go conference with the Ogres. In the end, it is up to you."

Kute watched his father contemplating his words.

Erosc toyed with his braided beard.

The new dialects baffled Kute, but this war was a more pressing matter. A better outcome should happen.

"Dionjor? Sifya? What say you?" Erosc asked.

General Umbala, taken aback, answered, "You know I am no longer Sifya, Father. Please respect that. I am now Umbala—whether you like it or not."

Erosc did not respond to his trans-son.

Uncle Dionjor tried to avoid his brother's misstep. "By Pyty, Erosc, we would look like imbeciles if we did not at least conference. Surely, this princess has shown a measure of diplomacy."

Kute looked at Umbala with a show of support. The transgender general grunted, scratching his sickle-lance. Slab jostled a bit.

"Well, I am glad someone is asking for my opinion." Fairy Queen Juna's head popped out of the furry bedding on Kute's jacket, her voice treble, youthful, and sarcastic enough to crack a smile upon Kute's face. She had lain in the fur, catching up on some much-needed rest. "I mean, who cares if we are two groups of people living in the same kingdom." The winds' current carried her shrill voice quite well.

Erosc sighed, prompting even Gravelp and Dionjor to crack hidden smiles. "Yes, Juna," the brash king's deeper voice bellowed, returning her sarcasm, "if we wanted a light show, we would certainly call you."

Juna jetted in front of Erosc, showing off her favorite cobwebby boots, wagging her finger at him. Kute tried not to smile, knowing she did not want anyone to outclass her in looking fashionable in battle gear. "Excuse me," she snapped. "You must be sitting on your head, Erosc, because you are definitely talking out of your—"

"Queen." Kute interrupted her before she completed her childish insult. "Queen," he repeated more softly, glancing warmly at his father and her, "it is a beautiful day."

"A glorious day," Erosc related.

"A demented day." Juna clucked and rolled her eyes at Kute, returning her attention to his father. "I agree with Kute and Dionjor. Yes, your people get their kicks off of war. My Ethnel, you could even become good friends with the Khunian Elves, but let us practice some diplomacy. What is going to be hurt by doing this?"

Erosc contemplated again.

Kute knew Erosc relished the war. The chance to show this neighbor his estate would not be trampled upon, that the Giants' valor reigned superior.

Diplomacy . . . now? This could be a good thing.

King Erosc grunted in disdain. "OK, I will listen to the majority opinion."

"I will go with a small party," Dionjor offered.

"No, we will all go with a small contingent to this unholy meeting." Erosc paused in thought before looking at Gravelp seated upon Hogar's Beard, her kiradoura. "And we will take their prized child with us as a show of decency. Would you not agree, Princess?"

Kute could see Gravelp felt awkward, as if alone in the Ty Desert surrounded by carnivorous Ty toads.

Gravelp pleaded, "You no . . . no understand."

"What is there not to, Ogre?" Erosc tried insulting her by not regarding her title.

Too weary to fight, Gravelp shrugged. She rubbed the opal pendant holding her silken cloak together at the shoulder, the few items left of her Ogrean identity wrapping Giantic fashion.

Kute rode Stonecrusher to her other side in a show of solidarity. "Father, can you see what an awkward position she is in? I will not have her treated as a pariah. She is a member of the Party of the Jode."

The sable-armored king stared at her, studying her.

"They come to war." She shifted in her seat.

Kute tried to stay above his father's scorn. "Father, may we proceed?"

The silence, too dense.

Erosc replied to his son, "There was a moment, Son, your mother and I were quite proud of you. This journey has taken something away from you."

"And it has provided me something probably greater, Father," Kute replied. "This does not mean I will not meet my death without the one Giant I have the greatest respect for."

Erosc's stern glare softened. He pulled on Shadocoat's reins, kicking the black pegasus's sides. The stalwart king led, flanked by four guards mounting large horses.

Like a puzzle piece breaking from its whole, the contingent trudged toward their profane meeting.

Juna nestled her Fairy form upon Kute's furred shoulder. "I swear, Kute, there are moments I am glad it was Ding who tagged along with us and not him."

"He is entitled, Fl-Fl—Queen." The prince tried to call her "Flower" in their dialect.

Glory to war.

Chapter 5: A Proposition

"It appears to be a strong one forming." I tested the air currents where we landed on Kyblore Island.

I did not need Khunian senses to notice this unnatural weather. Ding and I waited on the beach in the fog. I peered upward at the developing thunderheads overshadowing the descending suns. The fog's thickness made my surveillance difficult.

Claybreaker and Slateripper munched on grass farther inland. Their tired wings drooped a little. When we landed, we made sure they drank more than their fill before Ding tethered them to a tree.

Beyond, more trees dotted the landscape, with apparent mountains farther beyond. Kyblore Island did not appear any different from the mainland after all.

"Drat this fog," I complained.

"It will not let up, Elf. That is the way it is here." Ding plopped down with his axe's faceted head between his legs. He needed the rest as well, with all his frantic movements in the skyways. "We need to move farther inland before the weather worsens."

"Well, then, let us go." I winked.

"Drat you, Elf," Ding grumbled. "Can you not give a Dwarf a moment's rest?"

What could I do? Nothing in particular, so I plopped next to the master thief and his axe, Gore. "I do not think we are close to the Jode."

"How can you tell?"

"My jodepiece is not reacting. It should be pointing in some direction."

"Well, what can you expect?"

"What do you mean?"

"Maybe it is farther than we think."

"You are probably correct, Ding. Look at that. We are actually maintaining a conversation."

In one of Gore's faceted blades, I could see Ding's sullen face turn a bit sour.

"It does not mean we are . . . friends." He paused. "We are here for the same thing."

What he stated was not an arguable point. More importantly, I needed Ding to lead me to the Nixies' estate, and by the same token, I knew Ding needed me as well. Many of us could get quite lonely at the top.

"Ding, have you had any memorial awakenings?"

"M-memorial what?"

"Awakenings. Have any forgotten memories returned to you? Kute had one where he remembered his shield bearer, Alduur, was his actual lover. I have had several—like that tree creature, Tungloc, I told our Party about. And another where I met Mitral, the Gnomic chief. He was so pale, and I could not hear him, as if he never had his booming voice at all. And then there was my first encounter with my Steadfast."

Ding grunted. His fingers shuffled the grass. "Is that not your divine right?"

"No. My gift is telepathy. Retrocognition, past sight, belongs to my mom and only her. You know, come to think of it, my divine right did not protect me from Xurchon's possession. My jodepiece did. "

"What are you talking about?"

"In the Dark Plains. Remember when we were racing to the Ogrean estate?"

"Yes."

"Do you remember seeing me struggling and Kute trying to help me?"

"I remember seeing you struggling."

"That was me struggling with Xurchon trying to control me."

Ding just stared at me blankly. "I am an atheist."

I continued. "Yes, Ding, I know you are, and it does not bother me. I am sure there are Lorellian atheists. Anyway, Xurchon attacked me spiritually. The only good use my telepathy was against that was in taking full control of my jodepiece. Half my spirit, my humanity, is embedded in the jodepiece that now protects our Party—Gravelp and Juna included—because of my telepathy. If we did not have my jodepiece, we would all be in trouble.

"Us speaking like Man does not bother you?" I asked.

"No. Should it?"

"You did not answer my question, Ding. Have you had any awakenings?"

"No. Should I? Again, I am an atheist."

"Just asking. Remember when I told you I hated myself?"

"Yes. Before I started my suicide flight on that dratted pegasus."

"I had an awakening at that moment. So strange. It was so strange because it was not from my past. At least, not my personal past. I saw a female, a Khunian, in Quirmean clothes wielding Demonslayer by a fireplace. I could not understand it. Past sight belonged to my mom—"

"So maybe you are becoming your mom," Ding grumbled impatiently.

"No. No, this was different. This was another awakening, but so different. She was no Khunian I ever met before. And why would she be wearing Quirmean garb? Those Elves distrust Man. And why would she be holding my Welbern?"

"Well, it looks like you have got a lot to think about. Pretty much what you do."

"Ding?"

He grunted.

"Has there been any demonsia in your kingdom?" I continued.

"You mean like those Ogres turning into those snake creatures with fanged fingers?"

"Yes. Dicen."

"And they all have a strange tattoo on their neck's nape? A hood with a pair of dots?"

"Yes. I see you have been listening. The Dicen. Have you?"

"No." Silence weighed heavy on stubborn Ding.

I did not want to push anything further. "A Dicen attacked me on the cliffs over the Mous Strait that morning right when you flew ahead of me. I was able to avoid it with Gravelp's help, but I am very sure that Demon was Crumb's dead wife, Squish. It was like she came back from the dead to try to kill me. How? I think it was demonsia, which our Party discussed on our escape to the Giantic estate, when a person allows a Demon not just to possess them but to take complete control of everything to the point that they become them. Crumb and she were a team. I am sure of it. It is all so weird. Xurchon must be laughing somewhere. Are you ready to go?"

He grunted, clearly relieved my babbling had ended. "Whatever it takes. Let us go."

I grabbed his arm to pull him up. He snatched it away, using Gore's upright handle as support. My poor beleaguered companion paused, took a deep breath, and turned to our new pathway.

"It is important to go," he said with a sigh. "We will trek in the mountains' direction."

I followed him into the field of green. A forested barrier enclosed the grasses, blanketing a mountainside a few miles away.

"Hold," the Dwarven thief ordered.

Alarmed, I prepared to grab Welbern, my sentient broadsword. My Elvin vision scanned the forest for intruders. "What do you see, Ding?"

"The mounts—what are we going to do with them?"

"Ding, you amaze me!" I chuckled. "One would almost think you were the general. What a promising moment."

He grunted.

I grinned, remembering our first fight when he vied for leadership of our little group. "OK, General Ding, what do you propose we do?"

Ding's sullen look disappeared as he acknowledged my question. How refreshing. He seemed almost bashful and pleased. I did not remember seeing behavior like this from him before. "I . . . I do not know. We could usher the mounts back to the Giants' estate."

"That is odd. Then we would not have a way to transport. What would they do? Swim back? Do the Nixies have such mounts?"

"Well, yes, but—"

"I have a proposition for thy situation." Swen, my stowaway genie. Her telepathic voice,

music to my ears—or mind, for that matter. Since our first meeting on the road to Khun, her very presence took my breath away. How could she be the Princess Prodigy I encountered in her mist at the Ogrean estate when we escaped? How could she be two beings? She could not.

I wanted to try acquiring the jodepiece's power, but with my essence being shared among the others, I relinquished. "And what do you propose, almighty genie who seems to invite herself into situations?"

Love. Love wavered around my question.

Her nebulous gases swirled out of the boxy lamp dangling from my satin belt. The gases lifted her fragmented form aloft, sidling her about me with numerous spindly legs. Her cosmic eyelids blinked upward as she studied me. "I am only here to serve thee, Master Ygl; protect thee from all forms of evil," she rhymed.

"So what do you propose?"

"I will conceal thy pegasi. Hide them within the surroundings. It is a task taken gratefully to hide them from other beings." Her loose, silvery tresses dissolved into her murky nebulae.

"So be it," I agreed.

Her displaced, contoured fingers flexed at different angles; her gases snaked around Claybreaker and Slateripper. The runes floating in her disembodied bodice chimed. "Oh, winged mares, standing naked and bare. I conceal ye. Mesh with the air."

Crackle . . . pop.
Crackle . . . pop.

The air burst around the mounts in tiny translucent pockets—tiny pockets that increased and merged to reveal the rest of Kyblore's terrain on the opposite side. The pegasi were not bothered, indulging in their grazing, never aware of their sudden change.

Within moments, they vanished.

Ding grunted. "So it has been done." He continued through the meadows leading to the forest, with me following.

"Master Ygl." My genie's nebula still encircled me. "Please allow me to stay behind. The pegasi need to be cared for while ye are gone. If thou don't mind."

Do genies actually think for themselves? Maybe I had gotten this part of the legend wrong as well. "No, Swen. No, that is a very good idea, but how am I to counter any of Xurchon's minions without your help? My humanity has been split among everyone, including you, and with it, my jodepiece's power. I almost feel vulnerable."

"Remember, because of it and me, thou are hidden. The evil lord's minions may be stricken. Please drop the lamp in this place. Please allow me to stay."

Maybe we had gotten the legends wrong? "OK, you can stay, but when the stakes are high, I will need you to fly by my side. Look at that! You have gotten me rhyming again."

She smiled. I shied away, too attracted to her since our first meeting in Lorel, unhooking the lamp from my belt. No, she could not be the winsome princess. *You are so beautiful*. My thought slipped. Thalla, my deceased wife, came to mind. How ashamed I felt, despite what had happened between Swen and me at Mount Royale. "Oh, I am so sorry. I should have not said that to you."

"Thou has said it before; words with power cannot be ignored." She paused, her floating head angled downward, as if bashful. "The most elegant sound I have ever heard, the eloquence of thy words." So alluring, this genie, making me completely nervous. How strange a creature.

"Swen, what do you know of the Princess Prodigy?"

"When she is revealed, much will mend, placing the curse at an end."

A curse? Maybe the Jode's existence was a curse. Of course it was. "Swen, I have memory of a tree creature named Tungloc. Do you know anything about him? He could be a great ally."

My floating genie took to silence.

Interesting. Interesting, indeed.

"Elf, where are you?" Ding demanded in the foliage.

The dented lamp slipped out of my hands and into her murky billows. Swen did not go in.

Chapter 6: The Key

Emperor Rondo pored over the mystic war map in his throne room uneasily. Posted Demonguards awaited the next orders with patience, including outside his doors. His personal guards waited in the exterior halls.

The eerie map glowed and pulsated in the shadowy chamber, a gift granted by Xurchon as a fragment of divine omniscience. The dimness clothed Xurchon well as he resided at the map's opposite end.

"This map doesn't seem to be much help, Lord Xurchon." Rondo felt uncomfortable with the whole affair. "I can only perceive grand situations and not specifics. Are we even going to find where Ygl and his Party went?"

For sure, Rondo spoke true. He could spot the Forest of Khun's mystical barrier banding the Protectors' estate, terminating in the Cory Mountains' midst. He could see the Giantic and Ogrean armies gathering outside the mountain range in a field. A massive, amorphous blackness, the Death Mist, slowly crept in that direction. General Spenz's army marshaled throughout the Dwarven estate, administering Man's laws. Yet there were no signs of Ygl and his "Party of the Jode." Not even Xurchon, with all his power, could detect them. Disappointing.

Ygl & the Dwarf

"Everything will happen when due, Rondo."

"When? We're thwarted by Khun. You stated your power and this jodepiece wouldn't succumb to anything. That Zaendara would fall to Man's might and my public would come to love me as well as all Zaendara. And . . . and now Swen is missing. Stolen from beneath us. Demonslayer hasn't been retrieved . . ."

Gentle Xurchon examined the uncomfortable emperor. The shadows and mystic light cavorted delicately upon the walls and ceilings. "Patience, Rondo. Intolerance will be your undoing. Never question my abilities."

"I'm not. But I wish I could show you to the world. Show everyone that you are the one true god who'll lead us to salvation instead of these games."

"Are not games what Man believes in?"

"Yes. Yes, but not in this way."

Too many days had transpired since Khun's defiant stance. The minor Elvin rebellions hadn't been squelched since the disastrous news was broadcast, despite his hope they would be. So why hadn't the Forest of Khun attacked? If not for the Death Mist, he would've feared spreading his forces too thin.

"General Spenz is doing a remarkable job in the south," Xurchon soothed.

"I would not know, Lord. I haven't received word."

"Believe me," Xurchon assured him. "I can see him subverting the Dwarves with his divine right over music. A bit of the royalty has escaped. It doesn't matter. We'll soon get what we're searching for, and the Giants will fall."

Rondo hoped Xurchon's words rang true, and Rondo still had the initiative in conquering Zaendara.

However, nothing stayed certain anymore. He understood from the forces he had amassed in southern Lorel that some had witnessed a possible sighting of Jonas, his daughter. Could her best friend and she be amassing an insurgence against his rule? Could any of them understand that all he wanted was love? How could they not understand, with their selfish ways? The Nixy female upstairs was the only one who seemed to give the abandoned emperor love nowadays—if ever.

And she couldn't be trusted either.

No. The plans would go as intended. The Quirmean army increased larger and stronger at Fumi as his public heard of the threat to their emperor and felt wary of their Lorellian slaves.

No. The plans should remain the same.

Patience: the key.

* * *

Sama roused from her memorial awakening with a start.

In her dream, she recalled spinning in churning waves beneath gray skies, escaping three Nixies standing upon a distant shore, two males and a female.

Nixies? There goes that word again. I must be one.

Were they near? Were they far? The distance kept shifting.

These Nixies appeared different from her. Their scales' colors . . .

The violent waves swept her somewhere else fast, churning past tiny creatures in a new world, albino creatures with multiple wings. Feathers with no color.

Ygl & the Dwarf

Sama found herself crawling upon a different shore, surrounded by trees. A forest.

Lorel.

She did not know where to turn, but she noticed some enticing fruit she had never seen before trailing ahead of her, cutting a path north toward tree branches that seemed to motion to her, branches swaying farther from the fruits' direction, like a doorway to a new world.

Nearly naked, with pieces of cotton covering her bosom and privates, Sama followed the swaying branches for days, eating the fruity sustenance as the trees led her away from creatures that looked like her but were smaller, with skin like Man's and very tanned. Her eyebrows peaked and her heart gladdened, the creatures never saw her on their treks. She barely saw them, but they seemed to be hunting for something. The branches did their best to hide her from them. These Lorel Elves.

"General Ygl!" she heard one creature say, their young "general" riding a sleek monster shaped like a dragon but resembling a unicorn.

"Hold, Steadfast," Ygl ordered his mount.

Every morning, she awoke within a sheltering underbrush next to a fresh bag of vines holding more tasty fruit, something she had grown accustomed to. Someone protected her.

The nights were colder than the cool days. She fretted until she woke one morning under a blanket of tightly knit moss, which she kept as a shawl for her strange journey—another surprising gift from her mysterious benefactor. The next day, a tailored gown made of lianas lay next to her.

She arrived at a pond surrounded by firs, so quaint yet enticing, like the fruit. She missed Kyblore Island. The pond would be her new residence.

Kyblore Island. Hmm. . . was that where she was from? What a strange name. Bits of her memory seemed to surface in this memorial awakening, but not enough.

Each morning, she awoke with more fruit and other gifts, like brown lilies surrounding the pond.

"Taste them," a voice like moist soil encouraged.

Is this my benefactor? She glanced about but found no one. What was there to fear?

She tasted the lilies, letting the sweet sugar tickle her senses.

One day, a sickness overtook her, and a plethora of perfumed roses with whitish edges surrounded her.

"Taste. Medicine," the earthy voice encouraged.

She did, letting the willowberry permeate her body with health.

The next cool day, she encountered shrubbery festooned with flowers with blue-green striped petals encompassing maroon-green stamens. *These are the prettiest flowers.*

"Protection," advised the earthiness.

"She does not need the fervor flowers' protection." A fifty-foot sycamore erected itself, its voice, a thousand branches swooshing. "I am here to protect the Nixy."

Sama wondered why the sycamore appeared different from the firs, its blotchy bark contorting to something akin to a pearly male face peering from the seminaked canopies. Upon his head, a fruity headdress dangled, adorned with sporadic fronds and blossoms that should have fallen during winter's onset.

Fruit? Her fruit. Oh, her mysterious benefactor!

Her leafy protector slipped beneath the browning canopies with a crinkling and a rustling, appearing moments later the same size as her, with sinewy limbs resembling arms and lumbering fingers. Strong hands with lush overlays.

"The hydroyids have forsaken you. So have your Nixies. Shame on them," his voice swooshed.

"Hydroyids?"

"Do not worry, Sama. We were to be neutral, but the hydroyids know what is happening and fail to act. We all do."

The forlorn Nixy gasped upon seeing the tree creature up close. Her benefactor's peeling skin exposed a greenish-white and yellow surface. A part of her wanted to run, but where? She had already run away from the other Nixies for reasons unknown.

"Do not fear me, Sama. I am here to care. So are the humads, with their lilies and roses, but they are too shy. We were to be neutral like the arrogant aether.

"The pond will freeze soon, but do not worry. We are here. The hydroyids should never forsake you."

With a wave of rubbery fingers, he enlarged a nearby fir, thickening its trunk to thirty feet in width. The fir's anterior bark shifted into layered panels that swayed open, revealing an interior lit by the twin suns' radiance. "This treehome will keep you warm. We will convince the hydroyids to keep the pond warm for your fish."

She stepped through the layered panels, which reminded her of jellyfish. Warmth beaming from the sculpted apertures comforted her. "The aether? The humads? What are you?" Her eyebrows peaked again.

Her benefactor stopped. A smile creased through his light-gray bark.

Feet. His feet had fibrous soles.

That was all she remembered. *No, there was more. More.*

From within her custom-made lagoon, she leapt onto the furred rugs in her bedchamber. She wrapped her scaly body in a luxurious robe made of bear, grabbed her potted ivy from the mantel, and raced out the door.

When her tall frame passed through the threshold, her blue-green appearance transformed into the shorter blonde illusion Rondo had created to protect her.

A Nixy. I'm a Nixy! She thought to herself. *I'm these creatures, and they're me.*

She rushed down the halls to the nearest garden. A garden outclassed by what the humads had gifted her. No Quirmean garden could compare to the humads' wonders. Why was her pond barren when the mist captured her? Where did the humads' wonders go?

"T-T-," she stammered, trying hard to remember her benefactor's name, her eyes seeking what she couldn't find past the thick palatial structures' geometrical marble, impeding any sense of nature.

She dashed through the courtyard, past surprised nobles, up stairs and stairs and stairs, tripping on a few.

To the highest turret she raced, peering from its westward window. She didn't care where Emperor Rondo resided. He was of no consequence, likely in his temple, she felt sure.

Ygl & the Dwarf

From the westward window, she could see it: the Forest of Lorel, with its spacious land. Deeper south, she could see a lone triad of sequoia treetops forming a triangle. A woody tenement rested in the triad's center, supported by bridges.

"T-T-Tungloc," she finally uttered. "Tungloc the dendruid."

She looked hard for signs of the enigmatic sycamore with the spectacular headdress along Lorel's tree line. She found none in her foolish attempts.

She found nothing, but something found her: a whimper. A whimper in the winds—drifting from spacious Lorel? But this was no ordinary whimper. It carried a woodsy smell, fibrous charm, and fishy wit.

But the trees never spoke.

Unexpected tears welled in her eyes like magic. "Ryl." She caught her whisper, hoping nobody heard it in the passing breeze, pulling her potted ivy closer, ever so close. Sama the Nixy reeled upon the ground, bawling. *Ryl. My son's alive. Alive. I can hear his whimper in the breeze.*

Yes, there was more. Tungloc's feet had fibrous soles . . . like Ryl's. Like those of her hybrid son.

She inhaled a few breaths. *Are you his father?*

Chapter 7: Negotiations

Between the Cory Mountains and the Dark Plains
Early evening

Alduur, Kute's secret lover and shield bearer, was curious about this meeting between King Erosc and the Ogrean contingency being held amidst their armed forces. As easy as the breeze, he straggled after their squad behind Kute, with the Ogrean princess Gravelp to his left as their squad awaited the Ogreans' approach upon the manicured pasture. Advisor Dionjor mounted to Kute's left while King Erosc saddled before the quartet. A small vanguard aligned before their quintet, with General Umbala front and center.

An Ogrean host of thousands aligned behind its approaching contingency half a mile in the distance, almost obscuring the Dark Plains' tall grasses in the north.

A pacifist twice Kute's age, Alduur did not like the idea of war, which placed him in the Giantic minority, but he would not leave Kute's side for anything. Yes, it had upset him when Kute took the credit for a Pride parade Alduur had led before the homophobic Erosc's palace, but Alduur finally understood that Kute did it to protect him from death, having Erosc strip him of his duke credentials, making him Prince Kute's property.

Ygl & the Dwarf

He had wanted to quit after Kute tried kissing him at Kute's homecoming to stop an antigay brawl. The thought of being outed frazzled him. The painful paradox he carried: a gay movement's "heterosexual" leader with not enough courage to rise against his own self-hatred.

Maybe Kute had earned his courage. After all, Kute had outed himself in that instant to protect Alduur, the former duke of the Northern Plantation.

The two squads convened to parley. They lined up, staring at each other for who knew how long. Strange mirror images sizing one another up. The first party posed grandly upon their pegasi and large horses, brandishing sickles, lances, and sickle-lances. Their bronze-like armor and perfumes a stark contrast to their rival's sparse stony armor, shabbiness, and stink.

Their rival? Much, much darker in complexion, with wider nostrils, slouched upon esteemed gryphons and bear creatures with tortoise-like shells called kiradoura. The Ogres sported mace-clubs and lengthy chisels. Flapping silks protruded from the granite coverings.

Both sides raised their respective shields, triangular and oval.

Closest to the Ogrean princess Gravelp, Alduur witnessed her sadness; she tried hiding behind bravery's mask as she fidgeted, forsaken, upon Hogar's Beard, her kiradoura.

He knew she felt discredited on one side, untrusted on the other—not a good position for anyone who wants to broker peace. Something they shared, feeling like an outsider.

Fortunately, she was not the broker, a task delegated to her other ally, Kute, who aligned his pegasus, Stonecrusher, on his Ogrean guest's upper right.

"What are those markings on their bodies?" King Erosc muttered. His bejeweled black beard blended well with his pegasus, Shadocoat.

"T-tattoos," Gravelp said in her broken language. "It traditional for culture. R-royals have special ones."

Erosc grunted, regarding her tattoos' orange-and-white speckles frothing upon her neck's sides. Her tattoos circulated down her arms like a waterfall, peeking through her silk cloak's flapping. "I understand they transform your people into monsters?"

"That is not true, Father," whispered Kute.

Noticing the Ogrean approach, Erosc greeted his adversaries. "Lo." Erosc addressed the oldest, darkest Ogre, closest to his age and teeming with authority. "I guess you must be the leader of this band?"

"No band," the Ogre corrected, straightening his posture upon a hawkish gryphon as he secured his cloak's azure agate pendant.

A bulky Ogre and a dumpy Ogre were positioned on either side of their leader. The bulky Ogre rode a falconine gryphon closer to the leader's anterior, with his vanguard facing Umbala's. That Ogre, not as big as Umbala but bulkier, had to be the general. He would not relinquish his stare.

The dumpy Ogre rode a kiradoura.

Alduur edged his white pegasus, Powder, closer to Gravelp.

The leader continued, "These my people. I their king."

"Oh, 'King' Smush, I presume?" Erosc questioned.

"Yes. You?"

"King Erosc of the Giants. Come, let us speak. Why are we here? And remember, we already have a prisoner."

Alduur touched Gravelp's hand as she recoiled at Erosc's nerve, making such a dishonorable statement after calling her his adopted child days before.

"Father?" Kute and his massive brother harmonized with disappointment.

Smush replied, emotionless, "She no citizen. She no prisoner."

Alduur understood all too well what her father meant, and though quite upset by his statement, he knew she remained powerless to do anything.

"Stay calm," he softly muttered to Gravelp in his wan armor.

"What is the meaning of this?" Erosc asked.

The dumpy Ogre replied, with surprising verbal coherence, "Exactly what my father has stated, King Erosc. Princess Gravelp is a traitor to her estate. An exile."

"Father?" Gravelp begged; the rest of her question evaporated in a gasp.

Alduur clasped her hand tighter, knowing her shock and dismay outweighed everyone else's. No one could deny the hurt of her loss—her father's dismissal of his eldest daughter. Alduur thought about Umbala being dismissed by Erosc for being transgender.

Perhaps these leaders could be good friends after all.

Again, Kute came to Gravelp's aid. "It is unfortunate you have taken such a route against your own daughter. Whatever the princess has done has been for your people's benefit."

"She killed her own," the dumpy Ogre defended.

"I-I n-no do s-such thing, Crumb," Gravelp retorted.

Kute reinforced her stance. "I promise you, Advisor, the princess in no way performed such an act."

Alduur, older and wiser, observed Kute's passion for the princess, beaming with pride.

"Yes, you do, Gravelp. You do such thing," judged King Smush, his voice like crushed cobble as he adjusted himself.

Alduur understood Smush blamed his daughter for the deaths at an orphanage.

"No," Gravelp muttered.

Kute tried his best to stay positive. "That is all right, Princess. We know what really happened."

"This does not matter," Advisor Dionjor interjected from atop his green pegasus in front of Alduur. "We still do not understand why we are convening in the middle of a battlefield."

With a gaze as barren as the Ty Desert, King Smush answered, "Peace. Want peace."

The puzzled pacifist realized no one knew what to think of the Ogrean response. Alduur smiled inside. There was hope after all.

A giggle arose from King Erosc's murmured musing; a boisterous laugh followed, irking Alduur, who knew his former best friend best.

The Giants laughed along, except for Kute and Umbala, who remained transfixed upon the Ogrean general.

"Preposterous," Erosc exclaimed with clattering braids. "What preposterous game is this?"

"No game, Erosc," Smush rejoined.

"You sit before me with a grand army aligned behind you and ask for peace? You dare present yourself outside my kingdom to ask such a thing and say this is no game? You have marched so many miles to deliver such a preposterous message?"

"Then, is true."

"True that you would dare to think you could best Giants in the craft of war. The glory of war is always mine, barbarian."

Smush's hawkish gryphon squawked aloud. The winds rushed stronger. Storm clouds approached quicker from the southern distance over the Cories.

"Calm, Dune," Smush soothed his faithful steed, annoyed. "This conference over. We go separate ways. War begin? So be it." He maintained his stony gaze.

Erosc, in his gleaming tungsten armor, replied, "That will be the only agreement." Amorphous light shifted upon the darkened metal.

Satisfied with the outcome, Alduur focused upon Kute's mysterious club slung across his rippling back. The weapon tickled Alduur's psyche. That strange club—with the bumpy head and kiradoura-claw handle—belonged to Ogrean royalty. Why would Kute have possession of Ogrean regalia when the two races had never met until today? How did he get it?

A question worth asking too late.

Both squads, distrustful of the other, turned steadily and completely to the immense armies awaiting.

Chapter 8: Pitter-Patter

Pitter-patter.

The steady downpour fell with the building winds, playing a typical musical rhythm with the forest leaves. Water pellets smacking nearer leaves produced deeper sounds than the pellets hitting farther away. I almost enjoyed nature's unusual music; nonetheless, importance weighed heavy to find the Nixies as allies in this war against Man and the Jode. Wherever they were. The mountain's border loomed closer.

"Ding, I do not mind it so much, but it is starting to rain. How much farther?"

"We still have a ways to go."

I appreciated Ding's drive; he was working very hard to get us to our destination. "So what do they look like? The Nixies," I asked pleasantly.

The husky thief paused a bit, lifting his reddish-brown brows, providing me a rough side glance as we barreled through. I would have liked to use my telepathy on him, but he would have sensed me because of my essence we shared within the jodepiece dangling from my neck, an essence we needed to protect the Party of the Jode from Xurchon's prying eyes. I never felt comfortable invading another's privacy unless the need became dire. I guess my dad would be proud.

"Why ask? You have seen Nixies," he grumbled.

"I have never seen them. Some of Lorellians have witnessed seeing one."

Ygl & the Dwarf

Again, he paused. His breathing got heavier as the downpour's rhythm intensified. Small puddles splattered under our eager feet. Wetness seeped through my tunic's front. I gathered my cloak. Ding pulled his hood snugly over his head.

The leaves' chorus in the upper canopies greeted the shower's kiss.

"We have got to find shelter until this storm ends," I advised. "I am hoping it breaks by morning."

"I am getting tired. There is a cave colony yonder."

Caves? Great! I did not mind the rain. Quite the contrary, for us Lorellians, in essence, appreciated nature. Not as much as our Khunian neighbors, though. Maybe I should have reveled in this wonderful onslaught late in the day; it certainly made for the perfect break from this adventure's craziness and an exciting weather change.

The rain drenched the wavy curls on my sun-beaten face—unexpected joy. Oh, to exalt in this pleasure! I hoped Ding would take off his hood to experience this joy, but he did not.

We arrived at a twenty-foot clearing, the mountains ominous before us. A series of caves dotted their slopes and a spotting of hills throughout. Ding led us to a large clearing within the grouping. The rain pelted down much harder, as if to punish us for not enjoying it as a present.

"Oh, my Achal, I just love this!" I could finally understand the Khunian Elves' thinking, "This is incredible."

How peculiar. This secluded world of sporadic caves on rolling hills and popping mountains. I mean, if the Ty Desert was the "sea of sand" in Swen's riddle, this could be . . .

"Ding, this must be the 'hidden green.'" My joy could not be overstated.

"Oh, shut up and keep running, fool!" he retorted.

As we ran through the colony, the caves seemed almost endless. We could have taken shelter in the initial ones, but Ding insisted on running. I did not complain, enjoying the weather.

The caves' dotting expanded into a horizon's distance. Unlike the Giantic estate's homes, these caves formed at ground level or a little above.

Strange. Somebody would think the Nixies would be inhabiting these low caves, but I had yet to see any. Where were they? Not a Nixy could be seen. Not a Nixy could be heard.

My Dwarven ally and I crashed through our chosen cave's threshold in a mountain—or "shore," so to speak—falling exhausted on the irregular flooring spotted with patches of weeds and dirt. I made sure to snatch a pair of dry branches before our entrance. Ding cast Gore aside, falling to his knees. I knelt, sliding my back-scabbard off and placing Welbern aside before lying down to study the craggy ceiling. Alas, we might have found the Jode.

Normally, a run like this would not bother me, but I had been using much of my psionics to safeguard my thoughts from the Party because of Swen's spell of protection encompassing us, an attempt that took a progressive toll on me. Was it really a good idea to instill part of my humanity in my jodepiece as a safeguard against its entity? What if the sneaky entity found a weak link in my psychic armor? None of this mattered. What had been done had been done; changing plans would not be plausible.

Ygl & the Dwarf

I felt bad infecting Welbern with my jodepiece, but I needed to chop my jodepiece in half so that Oreol could use a piece to protect the Forest of Khun. I hoped my strategy worked.

And how about my memorial awakening on the cliffs over the Mous? Who was that female Khunian holding my blade? Who was she defying with grit? Who? How did she possess my blade? Blasmle spoke truth to me. Our historical scrolls had no record of her—whatsoever—and only my mother had the divine right to see the past's treasures, good and bad. These memories haunted me more and more.

"Ding, how are you?"

He paused. And paused again. How could I expect my Dwarven friend to step out of character? I had grown used to his hateful retorts. "I am fine, Elf. We should rest."

"I could not agree with you more."

Ding rolled flat on his belly. I curled up, wrapping my arms around my knees. He must have been more exhausted from his turmoil with Slateripper. I scooted next to the Dwarven heap, appreciating the pitter-pattering rain.

The forest's dampened scent seeped into the cave, reminding me of my home, Lorel. Before me, in the ensuing tempest, I could imagine Thalla and me dancing together, appreciating Miredo's blessing from above. Our son, Limbus, and Snip would come running, joining in our domestic merriment. I would turn, pick my son up, and spin him around—a family moment I had not experienced in a long while! I wanted it so badly.

A shadow would encircle my family and me, growing larger with each arc, trying to link to the shadowy path's tail end. The shadow would be

Steadfast, encircling us and landing beside me, producing a neighing roar with fire spouting from his flaring nostrils. My beautiful mount with his sinewy white neck. Yes. Yes, this moment I missed most dearly.

My closest knuckle rubbed moisture beneath my lower eyelid—moisture not from the rain. This cave's gloomy interior replaced the idyllic scenery outside. This almost tomb. This suspect foreboding.

Where were the Nixies?

Where was the Divinity?

Damn you, Achal. Damn you, Miredo and all the rest!

So . . . so very . . . weary . . .

I whimpered. I whimpered an oh-so-silent whimper, though I doubted Ding could hear anything with all his snoring.

How could you do this, goddess Achal? Abandon us? We needed you and Miredo and Istratos and Welna, Ethnel, Lolung-Cor, Henc . . . Where? Where were you?

A draft whizzed through the gloomy grave. I arose, wiping the tears from my face, gathering dry kindling for a fire with the branches I snatched. The wind must have blown much of it in. I created a small shallow crater next to Ding in the sparse grasses with my hands and ignited the fire with some flint I acquired from the Ogrean estate. Up and up, nature's smoldering miracle rose.

I grabbed some sticks to feed the flames, resting next to them. Soaked and resting inside this dimly lit cave was humbling. I had the fire going pretty strong. Tomorrow, our clothes should be dry.

Chapter 9: Fatherly Love: Crumb

Between the Cory Mountains and the Dark
Plains
Early evening

"What are you doing, Father?" Ogrean Crumb asked Smush.

"It what correct to do, Crumb," Smush said, answering his oldest child.

Crumb glanced back at the receding Giantic flank heading to its point of origin. "You cannot do this." The advisor's heart raced. "They will attack us from behind."

"They will not," his father reassured him.

"You cannot allow this to happen."

"Peace answer," Smush justified.

Advisor Crumb stared at the Ogrean king, his mouth agape. The resolve upon his father's face could not be mistaken. "So we are going back to our estate?"

"Yes."

"They will attack us, you know," Crumb insisted.

"No. Will not."

"I agree with Father." General Punok interceded against his older brother. "Desert intolerable to them. Look what wear." He motioned at the Giants' heavier attire.

First Queen Gasma stood firm upon General Punok's broad shoulder in a field of chimaera fur.

"Let them try, my friends. They will experience an Interim not even the Ty could offer. I would certainly like to take another shot at their First Queen again. She was fun." Gasma observed the departing Giantic envoy with a snicker.

"Do what want, First Queen," Smush replied. "We go home."

Los and Num's rays still provided some bright exposure where the grand armies positioned; Nus and Anul would soon arrive, bringing night's cover. The storm clouds' descent slowed. Los and Num would not be overshadowed just yet on this tense day.

Crumb fretted upon Patch, his kiradoura. *This cannot be,* he thought to himself. *Something must be done. Xurchon, I implore you. Help me. We cannot let this come to pass.* He stared at the tannish grasses scrolling past him, wondering about the circumstances' foolishness.

His attention averted to Patch's neck. Certain segments of the kiradoura's fur peeked out from between its shelling. Those segments commenced to move. Some clumped in a more linear fashion while other parts tilted away from the clumping, creating a word, three gradual letters: *Y E S.*

Crumb exhaled, relieved by Xurchon's unexpected response to the request for assistance. The moment had come. The evil Giants had to know who was superior. They had to pay.

First Queen Gasma twirled down to her seat, her leather boots lodged upon Punok's pilose shoulder. "What is the purpose?" She pouted, deciding a keen hope had been lost. "What a waste." Her tannish hair with blonde specks curled over her ample bronzed breasts as she leaned forward, twiddling his flecks of fur. Her arm's tattoo, taut, curvy lines.

Farther behind Gasma, a rear guard riding a black-and-brown kiradoura and brandishing a long, sharp chisel shuddered with widened eyes. His iris's brown darkened to black, a blackness eclipsing his sclera's white. He slowed his kiradoura to a stop, ordering it to turn.

An Ogrean comrade noticed the rear guard's odd behavior and stopped to investigate. The possessed guard immediately raised his weapon high, arching it.

"Stop!" his comrade yelled.

The weapon whistled into the air with a force never seen before—toward the Giantic envoy. A fearful silence enveloped the Ogrean group.

The blackness dissipated from the bewildered guard's eyes.

"What you done?" Smush asked, helpless to stop the careening missile already halfway to its mark.

Crumb sighed with relief. Yes, Xurchon had come to help at last.

Chapter 9.1: Fatherly Love: Kute

Between the Cory Mountains and the Dark
Plains
Early evening

Kute and the Giantic envoy proceeded quietly to their ranks, a quiet not sobering enough. In fact, the envoy's quiet leaned quite the opposite, relishing in national pride. Courage and honor, its prime ingredients. A hunger to reenact years of battle practice in the tourneys simmered in the mixture.

Kute thought differently from them, and he knew Gravelp and Juna would agree. He knew trickery and lies decorated this war under the guise of conceit. And certainly not on the Giants' part and maybe not even the Ogres'. Kute felt helpless; to the Giantic prince, war's glory had now come at a dire price.

At the same moment, peace's unexpected entrance into this foray was a welcomed reward.

His envoy's formation remained similar to what it had been at the conference, with one exception: Trans-general Umbala decided to command the rear guard with the other soldiers.

"Save your energy, Slab," Kute heard Umbala say to his favored war beast; assured, Umbala rubbed the rosy mane and wings.

The Giantic army awaited his envoy. Banners exhibiting tumbling fruits and vegetables flapped nonstop in the escalating winds, blending with the weapons' imagery.

Farther in Kute's background, he did not notice the mysterious thunderheads' hesitancy building and building into a cumulus mass over the Ogres.

"Did you really think that was appropriate, Father?" Kute asked Erosc.

"What?" the Giantic king rejoined. His bejeweled tresses glistened in the suns' light. Proud Shadocoat trotted upon razor hooves that dug a little too deep into the tanned grasses.

"With all due respect, I think it was rude to call the Ogres barbarians," Kute insisted.

Erosc rode stoically for a moment, never turning around. "Kute, I need for you to come forward." His son responded in kind, making sure to ride closer, knowing the brash king. "I need for you to side with me. Your mother is within the Cories, doing her best to assist and lead our people. I need you to assist me out here."

"Father, you know I would never leave your side. We are related," Kute assured.

"Much like Gravelp over there and her father?" Erosc challenged.

The Giantic prince slid a glance back at Gravelp, noticing her offense to his father's statement. Kute knew to stay calm during this dire state of affairs. "Father, the situation between those two is not what you may believe. I believe in the princess. Please believe in me. You already considered her a possible daughter."

Erosc paused for a moment in his ebony regalia, almost glowering. "It seems faith is all we have left to go by."

"This is true. You can see their king does not even trust the princess."

Erosc grimaced. "Yes, I can see. Maybe we did have it all wrong."

"It is not too late."

The loving king looked at his son. "Hmph. We thrive for the glory."

Kute felt at a loss. "Father, I do not understand you. These people have bravely stated they want peace. Why are you being so preemptive?"

"I do not trust them."

"So that makes us better to attack—"

"Before they do? Of course."

Kute argued further. "Then that makes us the barbarians, Father. It makes us no better. We can be better."

"If I may intervene—" Alduur remained calm in his debonair way.

"No, you may not intervene, conscientious objector," Erosc mocked.

"We were once best friends, Erosc," Alduur responded, unruffled.

Caught off guard, Kute tried intervening. "Shield bearer—"

"Not anymore, Alduur," Erosc retorted. "You should not have led a rebellion against my estate."

"That was a parade," Alduur corrected.

"And all those acts of aggression before that 'parade' were not rebellion?" Erosc continued.

Kute motioned his secret lover to silence, stressed that Alduur had almost quit. He knew Alduur would face possible death by Erosc if Kute had not pulled rank, forcing Alduur to remain under his wing. "Father, you must admit you were punishing a group of people for openly being who they were. You now know I am one of them, and so is Umbala."

"It does not make me feel any different about any of this. Especially when a heterosexual decides to help them out."

Kute knew Erosc was referring to Alduur as the "heterosexual." He aimed to keep his lover's secret. "I know this is not the place for this discussion, and I doubt you would reinstate my shield bearer as duke of the Northern Plantation anymore, but think about it. You would have a better army because of it. I am not any different. Neither is Umbala. My shield bearer only had the best of intentions, for us and the estate."

Again, Erosc fell silent. He took a puff from his briar pipe's long shoot. "What have your travels done to you? You are so hard to comprehend, yet again, you ring true."

"I have gone through much tribulation," Kute answered, perking up.

"And you have grown with it all, my seed. You will make a fine king"—Erosc grimaced—"once we figure out what has happened to our tongue."

"So you have changed your mind?" Kute asked, winking at Alduur.

"At the risk of angering Lolung-Cor, let the Ogres be the first to send—"

A whistling came fast and hard from above and behind.

Too fast.

Too close.

Kute had strong instincts, trained over many years at the tourneys, but he looked in shock as the speared chisel zoomed in slow motion through the group.

Kute noticed a thin trail of ivory smoke seeping from the focused missile.

Queen Juna, whose Fairy pores meshed with the air, launched from her perch upon Kute's shoulder, drawn toward the aerial disturbance.

"No." Kute's shock left him breathless. The chisel flew too fast—unnaturally fast—slipping past Umbala and the guards' shields.

And headed toward Erosc.

"No!" Kute screamed in earnest. The prince leapt between the missile and his father, calling upon his divine right, trying to double his body's size in the process. His quick response amazed him. Was this the help of his fraction of the jodepiece? No, the jodepiece's power had been reserved by Swen and Ygl for Kute's concealment. His burst of energy was one thing and one thing only: a child's immense love for his parent. Kute would not have Erosc harmed.

Juna shot a blast of white light at the impending danger. The chisel-spear split in two, continuing with its trajectory, leaving her divine right shooting between the beams.

Magic, Man's divine right, was at play here on the new missiles, yet not a Quirmean roamed around?

"Lolung-Cor, give me strength!" Kute screamed. With his enlarged right hand, he grabbed the nearest chisel's stem, crushing it. The second spear pierced his bronze armor and his upper-right abdomen, striking through his back. A pain he experienced in war games past returned, but this pain ran deeper than ever before.

Kute gritted his teeth.

The wounded prince bounced off Shadocoat's rump and onto the ground, reverting to normal size. He wailed.

Ygl & the Dwarf

As if the very air delivered her, Juna arrived, zipping about his head with a thousand apologies. "Oh my Ethnel, Kute. I am so sorry. I cannot believe what just happened. I had it. I had it! What just happened? Somebody help him! I had it. Can somebody help him?"

Umbala was the next one Kute saw rushing to him upon reddish Slab, then leaping off. "Keep it there, Kute!" the general ordered. "Do not pull it out."

Kute postured sideways upon the ground, his divine blood dripping from the weapon's pointed head onto his posterior. The chisel's shaft rubbed against his ribs.

He tried looking up at his father, but Erosc stared back at the Ogres. Kute imagined his father glaring at the Ogrean envoy, observing the scene, an unholy anger welling within Erosc. *Good thoughts. Good thoughts. Think good thoughts.*

Kute breathed heavily with nothing to say, glancing down, trying to keep himself upright with his arm, his fingers clawed deep into the tanned land.

A set of ivory boots appeared. Elegant Alduur.

Kute tried not to lament. His guilt rose. He wished he was not so ignorant about Alduur's efforts with the gay movement: protecting the LGBT who refused to be shield bearers for coming out, hiring them for the Northern Plantation, and protecting them from Erosc's ire. Alduur was right. Kute wished he had joined Alduur when the former Duke of the Northern Plantation led the Pride parade in front of Erosc's palace. Kute could have protected Alduur better. Maybe Alduur would still be a duke and not his shield bearer.

Alduur assisted in hoisting him from behind. A tiny dusty puff burst from Kute's upper body. Alduur, Kute's secret lover, the one he would protect above all else, now protected Kute from pain.

Two leather-strapped sandals decked with a pair of agate beads appeared next to Alduur. Princess Gravelp knelt at her friend's feet. He could see the helplessness in her eyes yet knew she was prepared to assist where she could.

Alduur pressed his forehead against Kute's bronze-like helmet, battle staffs at the ready. Confusion touched Kute as he remembered his shield bearer had wanted to end their relationship out of spite days ago. "Hold still, Kute. We have you," he whispered, acknowledging Umbala at the front.

"H-help me hold this in place, A-Alduur," feeble Kute asked, shocking his surrounding supporters. Kute rarely if ever stated someone's name, out of respect for their titles, and to state his shield bearer's . . . "Wh-why am I n-not healing?"

"Move," Erosc ordered the trio with a graveness that could pierce through any armor. His hefty left hand clutched his son's lower side, lifting the six-foot Giant high, his ebon pegasus kneeling for the retrieval. "Hands off my son," he ordered Alduur.

Fairy Queen Juna zipped about Erosc's head, admonishing him with a pointed finger. "Oh no, we are not going to have this attitude, Erosc. We have got enough problems without you bringing all this family drama. This is not the place. Fabia would definitely—"

"Father . . ." Kute quivered, trying to defend his graying lover, knowing Erosc ignored the "pesky" Fairy queen.

"Shh," gentle Erosc admonished his favored son. With the divine strength granted to him by

Lolung-Cor and Pyty, he hoisted Kute high above a rising Shadocoat.

"Father—" Kute tried to protest.

"Hold still," Erosc ordered. "Hold that godforsaken weapon in place." With a gentleness unknown, the Giantic king settled his son sideways upon Shadocoat's spine, assisting Kute with his right forearm so that the spear's point would not strike Shadocoat's neck.

As more guards encircled the grouping, Kute felt Erosc tremble.

"Father . . . " Kute tried to search for Erosc's brooding red eyes, denying a tearful welling. Red eyes only Ygl saw when Erosc really had blue eyes, but somehow, Kute could see the red eyes as well now—must have been Kute's connection to Ygl through Ygl's jodepiece.

The wounded Giant knew what was to happen. He would try to stop it regardless.

His resolute uncle, Advisor Dionjor, intervened in emerald regalia. "King Erosc, you know what must come next."

"On your call, Father." Umbala clenched his bejeweled horn, crafted from conjoined conch shells.

Erosc stared across the tanned field at his massive army stretching throughout the alpine range's border.

"Father . . ." Kute gasped with all the strength he could muster. "Believe in her. Believe in the princess."

Erosc kept staring, shocked, into the distance.

Kute glanced as best he could, continuing. "To all who can hear the sound of my voice! Princess Gravelp is to be protected! She is in league with us. Do you hear me, Father? If this is to be my final day, let these be my final words. Believe in Princess

Gravelp!" Kute grasped his father's shoulder. "Do you hear me? Believe in Gravelp as I do. Protect the princess, for she will protect you. Do you hear me? Let these be my final words."

Umbala and Alduur straddled beside her, fulfilling Kute's demand.

"You pacifist?" he heard Gravelp whisper to Alduur.

Alduur did not flinch, scratching his graying sideburn, pulling his battle staffs from their posterior sheaths with elegance. "Yes, I am, but I will defend when I need to. Defend. Never attack. And young Kute needs me as more than his shield bearer now."

King Erosc grabbed Shadocoat's reins, acknowledging his former best friend's words. "What is said by Prince Kute is as shall be done."

"You heard what has been ordered," Trans-general Umbala emphasized to those closest. "Spread the order quickly. Widely. Now!"

Juna dashed her three-inch frame into the middle of everything with importance, the winds carrying her voice with gusto. "By my wings, you heard them! Fairies, spread the word."

Umbala pressed his imposing horn against hulking lips. A commanding blare resounded from the shell's deep recesses, an impressive Nixy import crafted by Dwarven forgery.

In response, a resounding wave of horns trumpeted an answer, echoing throughout the mountaintops. Much like that echo, the large horses' powerful hooves barraged through the tanned field at the Ogrean threat. The colorful pegasi took the cavalry farther into the skyways. An ominous, sparkling flood of Fairy warriors ballooned upward like a mushroom cloud, darting across, ahead of the Giantic forces.

The thunderhead that came to a standstill above the Cories began rolling inland—faster.

"Hold still, Kute," Erosc ordered as he reared Shadocoat into the sky. He grasped the shaft on Kute's anterior more firmly with his right hand as he steered with his left, his divine strength also bracing his son. Kute held on to his father as best he could.

Stonecrusher followed his beloved master. The loyal equine needed no orders.

Chapter 10: War!

The tan field
Evening

King Smush's heart sank as he witnessed the speared chisel hitting its mark. His heart sank further when the missile seemed to split into two pieces. And his spirit sank more when his rear guard kept repeating, "It not me, great King! Something took hold me. It not me!"

Smush's heart throbbed slowly before rapid beats set in. He perceived Crumb, his oldest son, with a new awareness of distrust. All hopes of peace—gone.

Smush stared at his cunning son, expressionless, as the massive Giantic military raced toward them. "How you wife, Squish, really die?"

"Protect King Smush!" Crumb yelled, reciprocating the stare. And his call reverberated throughout his envoy as everyone veered their mounts against the Giants' quickening approach.

A shocking thunderhead formed, rolling with the swarming Pixies who focused upon the Fairies.

Another astonishing nimbus evolved midfield. Distant thunders rumbled.

Smush's youngest son, General Punok, postured. "We braver than think, Father."

Upon the battlefield's opposite ends, a similar scene played. Smush and Erosc fled through an onslaught of two Faerie forces, warriors, and winged cavalry. The kings fled from shame. Shame of betrayal. Shame based on confusion while fervent soldiers converged to protect pride.

The Faerie armies collided with each other with a clash of swords and scissorlike fluttering, wings darting.

The other airborne forces followed the tumultuous encounter with gryphons' roaring squawks and pegasi's voracious neighs.

No matter how loud and eager the air battle, nothing could surpass the engulfing ground forces barreling upon each other. Kiradoura claws and razor horseshoes lashed out at their intended targets. Hammers and chiseled spears crashed upon breastplates and bronze shields. Lances and sickle-lances eagerly sought openings in granite.

"Sand suckers!" Giants insulted their opponents.

"Mud lickers!" Ogres slurred.

The three thunderheads rolled and merged into one nimbus as the buffeting winds built and built. Forked lightning flashed over the shadowed terrain.

Chapter 11: Count Them

I raced through the blackened space in my dream.

What was I running from? I had no idea. I just knew I had to keep running and running through the void. Alone. In empty darkness. Was I in the Interim, the dimensional world of horrors even Demons feared? I witnessed no shadowy land below me, heard no Demonic screams. Yet I knew a threat existed and did not know why.

My Achal, I fell! Yet I did not. I had to be in the Interim.

An eerie fullness in my gut awoke me, spreading throughout my limbs, making me more connected to something in this void. Not just any fullness. It felt empty yet complete.

"Ding? Ding, where are you?"

Where did he go? The fullness kept pulling at me through the blackness. I could have fought it, but I knew I needed it. I almost craved the fullness. The energy was essential, and so I followed the fullness, against my better judgment.

My heart felt like a frightened rabbit ahead of me. My breathing, faster.

I should not be here.

My sword—where was Welbern?

In an instant, I found myself zipping through this void. A force pulled me, the fulfilling energy thrilling me.

A part of me returned. Had someone in the Party met their end?

Ygl & the Dwarf

My answer appeared, hazy at the spiritual beacon's end: a stocky, stubby answer with a lengthy beard glaring at me with Gore at hand.

My jodepiece rested on his other.

Somehow, I needed to look up. Two pairs of five-foot pupils sized me up on both sides. The eyes' outside corners slanted upward. These were not Vantenian eyes from Quirm—they were Elvin!

"Achal? My goddess, is that you?"

One pair of eyes could have belonged to my goddess, but the left pair looked different. Their irises emitted a beautiful green, as deep and glittery as the Urvan Sea. I could almost fathom clinking scales beyond the mysterious pairing, bluish-green scales.

Who was this?

The visual quartet seemed to speak, though I could not hear them. The left eyes furrowed—an admonishing voice packed with graspable dreams blared from them. The other eyes' voice, more caring, bubbled with countless memories.

"Wake up," they warned.

I did.

Above me, the infinite blackness disappeared. In its place, the ceiling of craggy rocks I was familiar with before I fell asleep. A couple of frightened bats flapped by. Moist foliage pervaded from outside.

Oh, my Achal. This embracing fullness still felt very real to me despite the dream, and I realized where it originated.

"Ding . . ." I mumbled. He rejected my spirit's protection! The returning fullness—my spirit mixed with a bit of his. This dream was real? He must have rejected Swen's protection as well.

I grabbed for my jodepiece on my leather necklace—gone!

I jumped up, realizing the worst had happened. Ding had betrayed the Party by stealing my piece! Kute was right. A thief was a thief after all.

Ding straggled out our cave's entrance with smoky tentacles in his fringes as the Death Mist entered around him. Absent anyone's magical protection, Ding writhed against my piece's might.

"Ding, you fool!"

He struggled and struggled. I did not need to imagine his pain. He raised his arm up, shouting, "I have the jodepiece, Xurchon. I have delivered the Elf to you. Can you not see him? Now, please. Please! Deliver me from this torture!"

As Ding turned in his frenzy, he seized my sword.

"Welbern! Demonslayer!" My telepathic sendings called.

The milky mist enveloped the quivering thief as he fell to his knees. But even as the mist had, Welbern vanished under my jodepiece's protection. My piece vanished as well, though Ding held on strong.

Welbern's low humming revived.

The Death Mist, with its bluish-yellow spangle, crept toward me. Defenseless, I did the only courageous thing I could imagine—I fled deeper into the cave's bowels.

Nonetheless, my spangling opponent proved too quick for my nimble feet. The mist's tentacles slithered so fast.

All I thought about was my first encounter with the Death Mist at my Forest of Lorel's spring dance, how it encompassed my Lorellians so rapidly.

How valiantly many kin fought. How we were captured. How my loyal Steadfast disappeared. And how Methelo, Rolando, Sylvia, and my beloved Thalla met their deaths.

Rondo and Xurchon's mist tried to wall me in the cave. This Death Mist, their instrument that housed Xurchon's Demonic children, which captured Ding and my kingdom. How many more estates would fall? I hoped the Forest of Khun fared better.

"No! You shall not have me, mist. You will not win! I have defeated you before!" My telepathy searched my milky opponent. Demons cackled and hissed in response. I reached for any mind within my mental proximity. A gremlin's cackle shortened. An imp shrieked in disbelief. My psionic sending searched within their dirty, soured minds' recesses, tearing them asunder.

Hand-to-hand combat was not beyond me. My infravision—Elvin ability to see warm-blooded objects with red auras and cold-blooded in blue—may not have been able to peer deep into the ethereal mess, but it could see what traveled inches before me. Like my enemy, I would harbor no quarter. However, the more I fought my unseen foes hidden in the vapors, the more the mist encased me, blocking my escape route.

A thin Demonic sword-arm, dripping with mangy fur, plunged at my waist. I leaped up, grabbing the scaly wrist as it passed underneath me. My feet stomped hard on the arm's elbow. Somehow, that stomp held unnatural power, shattering the joint on the ground as I ripped the surrendered forearm from its housing, providing me two weapons: a crude sword in one hand, a shocked open claw in the other.

My knee blinded a mini-Cyclops coming into view.

A rusty broadsword sliced through my ankles like butter before decapitating me . . .

I took a deep breath.

What had happened?

My head somehow remained on my shoulders. The mist still surrounded me, the cackling and hissing accompanying it. I found myself still standing. I needed to reassess what had just occurred—and quickly. By instinct, I leaped up; an axe swept below me. Again, by quicker instinct, I lowered my head. Another broadsword swooped past me from behind.

By the Divinity! My goddess, Achal, blessed me with Advisor Sylvia's gift of forethought, the ability to foresee anything in the near future. I found myself running in a particular direction. I did not know what direction. I just knew the way was correct. If a rock or any obstacle impeded me, it did not matter. I knew the obstacle was there before I got to it.

What a wonderful gift, precognition. Why did Sylvia not use her divine right before Man's assault on Lorel? She could easily have warned us better than I could. Or even my brother, King Methelo, for that matter. What had taken place? How could they have allowed such a horrendous event to happen to our forest and Zaendara? Why? They met their deaths because of their failure. It made no sense.

No sense. No sense, unless—unless they meant for Man's invasion of Lorel to occur.

My stomach soured as I dodged the Death Mist's assailants' constant barrage. How could Methelo do this? How could my own brother and

Sylvia do this to me? To Lorel? There had to be a reason.

Not a moment could be wasted pondering this notion. Amazing, a disastrous fate had not met me yet.

A humming.

I heard my blade's familiar sound, like a gathering of gentle bees. *"Welbern! Come to me!"*

Demonslayer's humming resonated louder through the Demonic chattering. Why had my sword not come to me? Maybe the mist had an effect on my blade. In any case, this broadsword and hardening claw would have to do.

I had to escape.

My feet's unnatural power, which had helped me shatter the Demon's elbow, pushed me off the ground.

Lifting. Flying! Climbing into the air in a forward motion, spinning, yelping, and slicing away at my attackers.

What was happening?

But my aerial climb differed from my experience at the Ogrean estate, where the air melted away from me with my jodepiece's touch, granting me entrance into space. This current miracle could not be magic at work because Ding owned my piece.

No. My goddess had delivered me another blessing: Prince Rolando's divine right of telekinesis—the ability to move anything with my mind. I felt quite awkward using my nephew's gift.

Of course, the mist did not ease my fear of running into a pointed rock. On the other hand, Sylvia's divine right provided instinct enough to avoid such obstacles.

Where was I headed? I did not know. I only knew my instincts had to take me there.

Fighting so many seemed almost futile. Surely, despite my new divine rights, I could meet my death. And what could I do when I did? How could I defy fate? My fate. Impossible. Yet fighting on was what I had to do, along with, I guess, believing I would survive this trial.

I flew, spinning and cycling, letting my clairvoyance and telekinesis guide where they could, still using my telepathy to mind blast whomever. Psionics at their utmost.

Where I was headed? I did not know. My clairvoyance led the way, which I knew was not outside.

The sentient mist performed its best efforts to keep pace with me. I began to tire, executing so many newfound tasks at once.

Yet. I. Must. Fight. On.

Then, the enigmatic Princess Prodigy appeared to my right, blinking in and out. I had encountered her in Swen's mist at the Ogrean estate, her eyes flashing bluish-yellow sparks behind the blurriness veiling her face. She waved me forward.

I dropped.

What just happened?

I did not feel a vacuum, like when I traveled in the Interim. This phenomenon, strange indeed.

Where did my new instincts lead me? Or my telekinesis? Or both? It definitely was not the Prodigy!

I envisioned a dagger stabbing my left leg— I winced at the slicing pain when one did.

Fatigue started setting in, lessening my reflexes, but the mist began to taper from me. My telepathy built, countering with a blast from my mind's core. A brief attempt, indeed.

Ygl & the Dwarf

I tumbled through the thinning mist into a voluminous blackness. The flashing Prodigy waved me along, her snowy hair whipping the shades.

But the fiends would soon be upon me with a drooling appetite. I had to think fast as the mist struggled to keep up. The fading mist's lightness grew denser. The chattering and chittering climbed.

You will not win.

Hungry Demonslayer's distant humming built with the not-so-distant screeching and yelping of Welbern's Demonic prey.

I relaxed and let go, releasing my will over my newfound psionics, letting my fall's force take me. Somehow, my psionics seemed to remain in control, taking me in a more diagonal route.

Baffled, I curled into a ball while holding on to my crude weapons, searching for any psionic reserves within me. My Soft Winds meditation triggered, the musing so unnatural against the gathering of so much reserved energy.

Calm. Stay calm. Hypnotic soft winds coursed through my bones . . .

My goddess Achal, I hurt so much from the body aches and trying to contain my left leg's bleeding with telekinetic energy.

An axe displaying a strange skull on its head sliced through my stiffened Demon claw. I jettisoned the rest of the grotesque arm toward my unseen opponent, leaving the swishing broadsword in my possession. This mist hid my many opponents well.

"Welbern, come to me. Now!"

A rattling threatened my right ear.

From my body's angered core, a psionic spark radiated to my skin's surface, pulsating. Psychic energy blossomed about me into a psionic sphere, blocking various weapons. My internal reservoir provided the bit of drive needed for the sphere—quite efficient, as long as it was not my jodepiece's wicked coolness. My sphere's energy built faster than the threat pressing on my bubble.

I fell and fell farther.

The flashing Princess Prodigy kept pace beside me, waving me in the same direction, her golden dress flailing.

My psionic bubble burst from the surge, jettisoning me away from the Death Mist's grasp. I shot my deadly cargo into my enemy, thrusting back a screeching Demon with mouths for eyes.

I found myself shooting through space at such a thrilling speed. My skin enveloped me in a thin shield, protecting me from any danger. I think Rolando called it a "skin-shield."

Thank you, Achal, for granting me these divine rights. Thank you.

The mist soon trailed miles behind me. Why did it stop? Could the mist be fearing the "power of the mountains"? But that adage stemmed from Kute's estate, miles across the Urvan Sea.

"Demonslayer. Welbern, come to me! Come to me now!"

My speed slowed, settling my fatigue. I hoped my landing would arrive soon in this bleakness.

The Princess Prodigy faded away, echoing her mantra from the Ogrean estate: "Answer my riddle. Find the Jode. Understand me. Know me."

It was so dark, but a pale-blue radiance flickered faintly not too far away, directing me to a site. Maybe the cave was a long tunnel opening on the other end?

Was this what Advisor Sylvia saw? Visions like this? Me fighting desperately in a cave's chasm, alone? Fighting within a mist of whiteness against an impossible foe? Maybe she did envision this and sacrificed herself for this moment to pass. Maybe she knew the fruitlessness of defying her demise at Lorel. Maybe.

I had to fear this vision. When would my life end? I could not dwell so long on this. What good would my ambivalence do with a more pragmatic situation at hand? I must admit, though, I had been beating my demise thus far.

As I closed the gap between the site and me, the pale-blue light seemed to move and direct itself to me. What was this phenomenon?

My Achal, how can I fight again when so depleted?

Too much. This was too much.

Achal, grant me strength.

So tired. So tired. I had to let go and let myself fall wherever my instincts allowed. I diverted my newborn psionics to my feeble skin-shield to soften my landing.

I fell, and as I did, the spooky light seemed to follow. I curled myself into another ball, bumping hard upon the ground. I prayed for no pointy rocks.

With each bump, flashes of my failures resurfaced. My lost kingdom. My lost family. My lost wife. My lost unipegon. My lost control over everything.

Jagged rocks tried to pierce through, but I felt quite cushioned. I crashed on a pair of thick, pointy rocks, suggestive of the manticora's mangled teeth that tried devouring me at Man's Torture House. The impact upon hitting the vertical rocks, too much. My skin-shield dissolved, flipping me sideways onto my back. I rolled onto my stomach.

The spooky beam followed me but did not seem to stay in one spot. Left then right. Up then down. Maybe the shifting illuminated the underground roots' shadows, but the shifting stayed on my perimeter.

I whimpered into an angry cry. My Achal, everything just seemed so futile in this void.

Alone. What was I to do now?

I peered at the light encircling me through welling tears, the shifting beam moving more than ever at the fringes. Was it growing larger?

My tired eyes glanced up, seeking an escape route. The pale-blue light shifted more, growing. Was there someone, or something, there?

Hopeless . . . so tired . . .

Chapter 12: Battle on the Tan Field

Outside the Cory Mountains

Thunder rolled and lightning flashed in the late-night skies. Torrential downpours greeted belligerent armies. Eager power pulsated between the troops as Giants fought to overcome the Ogres.

Fifteen-foot banners swayed upright above the heaving masses. A set of triangular banners exhibited a jumbled array of fruits and vegetables. The oval banners, a rigid network of stones. If a banner fell, a new bearer hoisted it. Ardent training gave the Giants an advantage at the conflict's start.

As the opposing sides slashed and bashed in the muddied field, Trans-general Umbala's conch shell arose somewhere at the marking where the battle was and where it was yet to happen. As his Giantic army pressed forward, a staccato tune filled the atmosphere of grit and zeal.

He blared a different sound, long and hard: a staggered line of Giants receded, signaling another line of sickle-lances forward, large horses and foot soldiers lunging into the susceptible Ogrean ranks. Surprised and wounded, the Ogrean line retreated— a little.

Umbala grinned a calm grin. His military strategy embarrassed and angered a particular Ogre wearing a cloak made of chimaera skin with a matching helmet. *Yes, the one who would not stop staring at me at the failed summit.*

The Ogre kicked his aquiline gryphon's sides, directing the mighty beast to the weakened arena. The eager mount squawked and swooped downward, talons flashing. The defiant Ogre raised his bulbous club and chiseled spear, equaling his mount's wingspan. *The bulbous club Kute owned? This Ogre is royalty!*

The Ogrean warrior struck with aggression matching his opponents', holding quarter for none. No Giantic weaponry fazed him. His chimaera cloak garnered some respect.

"Onward, Pillager!" the Ogre ordered his mount.

The gryphon proved just as voracious, swooping and diving past aerial assaults, barreling into the Giants' line; the massive wings bowled over and wounded many along the way. His clawed forepaws delivered as much damage while his leonine hind legs picked up a foe or two, thrusting them into the fray. Together, rider and mount practically devastated the Giants' new offense.

General Umbala steered Slab near; he pounced upon the gryphon's lower back. "Very impressive, barbarian. I suspect you must be their best warrior." His lance shattered against Punok's invulnerable skin. The pieces scattered in the increasing winds and rain. *What?*

"I more than that, monster," the mighty Ogre challenged, trying to swipe Umbala's feet, but Umbala would not budge. "I General Punok." He kicked the gryphon's sides for a quick jostle, unbalancing Umbala. "I more than best warrior." Another jostle and swipe were sufficient to knock the transgender general off. Punok leapt after him. "I their lead warrior! You suffer my hands!"

Umbala struggled hard against his smaller, worthy adversary with skin of brass. He seized Punok's spear within his sickle-lance's jaw, thrusting it out of Punok's grip.

Punok was quicker than Umbala had thought. The Ogre flipped around and pounced upon Umbala with foot-long boots of granite.

The force would have immobilized the massive Umbala, but the Giantic general twisted Punok beneath him.

A ring of Giantic warriors protected Princess Gravelp and her kiradoura, Hogar's Beard. From behind their defense's second line, she could not tell who was winning within the raging storm. Especially between the Pixies and Fairies, which prompted a disgruntled Fairy contingency to surround Gravelp as well.

She shuddered at the Fairies' angry looks, her silken cloak not very good protection against those either. She grasped more tightly to her kiradoura's tortoiseshell, sighing with relief at her mount's presence.

Anyone would believe the Giants had the advantage, but the Ogrean princess knew that her race's existence in the harsh Ty Desert granted Ogres much perseverance.

"Are you one who command group?" she asked a guard mounted upon a yolk-colored horse in front.

Drenched in rain, the seven-foot guard studied her with no disdain. "Yes," he answered. "General Umbala has asked my squad to protect you."

"I want help," Gravelp replied.

"You want to help?" He hunched down.

91

"Yes." She tried wiping the rain from her wet face.

"Well, that is not possible."

"Why?"

"Because I am to regard you as I would the prince, and that is what my squad and I intend to do."

As they spoke, Gravelp witnessed the Giants' elegant pegasi swerve past the Ogres' rough gryphons. She marveled at the well-trained pegasi; however, the gryphons' prowess was a competitive asset. When the different mounts collided, their riders held no remorse for each other or the splattering rain.

Farther away, she witnessed one of the largest gryphon riders barreling down upon the masses. The damaging duo disabled any Giant obstructing their way. No weapon could harm the rider.

"Punok," she whispered, alarmed. "Please, sir. You allow me to go. I see my general there. He my brother. His divine right invulnerability. Skin and bones very hard."

Advisor Dionjor chimed in from her right. "That is OK, Gravelp. General Umbala has immense strength." The mounted advisor sat tall upon the well-armored Caldera. His breastplate resembled a maple leaf with its frilled edges.

"S-Soon my f-father and Crumb arrive." Gravelp palmed the pink agate attached to her silk cloak, almost as if hiding her embarrassment. "What have against such power?"

Dionjor smirked. "Mine is the divine right of fertility and abundance."

Gravelp shook her head. "Not enough. They powerful. I must participate." She fidgeted upon Hogar's Beard's shelling.

Ygl & the Dwarf

The calm advisor stared at the Ogrean princess for a moment, replying, "This is not a participation, Princess. It is war. And you underestimate me. I am a warrior like the rest of my race. Do not let my frail appearance fool you—or my divine right."

Gravelp became impatient, trying to measure her words. "You. . . need. . . m-me. I no care—aah!" A deep slash ripped into her upper-left leg. Yet she saw no wound. No gory cut developed where the insistent pain festered, no blood for the rain to wash away. *This must be connection to Ygl through jodepiece. Please, great Hogar and Falvanch and his Achal. Please protect him wherever. Poor, poor Ygl.*

What is this? Juna, the Fairy queen, thought to herself as she swerved to avoid a watery blast from the liquefied Pixy queen, Gasma. Juna's white light sparkled in one hand as she searched for a dart with the other. Fairy skin was quite porous to air but not to water, especially in this freakish weather. Where had the suns gone?

Watery Gasma chided Juna. "What is wrong? You cannot handle a little shower?" She hurled herself at Juna. "Did you pull a leg muscle?"

Juna nimbly dodged the sentient jet stream, her white light obstructing watery blasts. She zoomed from the Pixy Council's laughing First Queen.

And there they hovered. Regal, three-inch Faerie fighting each other: trendy Juna's paired wings versus sleek Gasma's quartet pairing. Juna knew they harbored surfaced historical contempt. What was that historical contempt? She did not know. And did not care.

She just knew that someone had to win while she dealt with the unyielding pain she sensed Gravelp was experiencing as well.

This rain really messed up her Aphronior bodysuit.

"You will not win!" Ygl's telepathic challenge rang through.

"Ygl?" Juna asked, caught off guard. *Of course, Ygl's jodepiece combined with Swen's protection spell still has all of us in the Party of the Jode connected. Oh, Interim no! This is messed up! But we definitely need to hide from Xurchon and Rondo. Ethnel, please guide Ygl's luck. I really do not need a nasty spear sticking through my chest. Especially in this outfit.*

The thunder boomed.

The lightning flashed.

A wide beam of the blackest light shot up from below and past Juna, striking sneaky Gasma before she took advantage of Juna's distraction, sucking her in, striving to tear her apart in its vacuum. She shrieked in bewilderment within its bleakness, a darkness nullifying anything.

"Burn her, Juna!" Juna's husband, Ood, in his designer chiton, tried maintaining his black light in the hammering storm.

Juna concentrated her divine right into the most brilliant light burning from every vessel in her hands, casting it into her husband's dark beam, which absorbed it.

Gasma shrieked louder, angrier.

The rain pounded harder. The winds buffeted stronger.

Like the Pixies, the patriotic Giants truly engaged in the game of war, whereas the Ogres and Fairies perceived this event as a travesty that should have never been. Nonetheless, war was waged: one group strangely exhilarated; the other, more fervent in demeanor.

"Welbern! Come to me. Now!" Ygl's telepathy bounced around to Kute, Juna, and Gravelp.

Liquid Gasma nipped out of Ood's black light, quite smaller in size and larger in anger.

As the stormy torrent fell, the exasperated Pixy queen absorbed the droplets, attaining her regular size.

King Ood slammed against Juna, knocking her away from a hard stream of dense bubbles cast by Pixy Queen Hoodia of the Pixy Council. The bubbles burst and singed a Fairy's wings and a gryphon's side, making both fly awkwardly in pain. "Are you OK?" Ood asked, his hair's straw highlights mussed in the winds.

"Yes. I have this pain in my leg," Juna answered her husband.

He examined it. "I do not see anything."

"That is because it is the Party's connection to Ygl through his jodepiece. We feel his pain. He is in trouble."

First King Guisarrio, Gasma's husband, advanced. Belts of rainwater cycled around his clenched fist. Pixy Queen Hoodia hovered next to him. Dense bubbles ballooned about her red leather gloves.

"Look. You cannot hope to defeat us in our element," the First King sneered to the Fairy couple.

"Your element?" Juna smirked.

Ood and Juna clasped hands as they witnessed Gasma expand in aquatic size; a firework of black-and-white light sparkled from their union.

Juna sneered at the Pixies' challenge. "I sure hope your ears are clean because I have got some good gossip here for you. And here is what it is: I do not know what you are feeling, but it is not happiness."

"This is not your element alone, barbarians," Ood added. Their threatening light spiraled about the pair, expanding with fury.

"Let us get done with round two, dung," Juna challenged. "And maybe after we kick your butts, we will teach you how to wear better outfits. I mean, have you never heard of Aphronior? Thoreus? Of course not, idiots."

The royal couple launched at the Pixy Council members, lights a-blazing.

Chapter 13: On the Mend

The Giantic estate
Southern region

The storm brewed wilder in the early morning. The twin moons, Nus and Anul, tried poking through the crowding thunderheads.

"Get some more elixir," Queen Fabia ordered a nurse. She maintained her composure as she observed her wounded son lying sideways on the infirmary bed in her refuge, half-naked, with a blanket over him. The Giants always had an alternate plan. Having a second home in the southern Cories, nothing new. The Ogrean weapon still pierced Kute; the longer ends broken for Kute's easier entrance. He breathed heavily.

She observed somber King Erosc standing aside, watching her touch their favorite son—their only son, as far as he was concerned—replenishing Kute with divine abundance.

His beard's jewels glistened in the light from a nearby fireplace. "I know how aghast you must feel, my love." He wanted to approach; he could not.

"Shh," Fabia responded with tenderness. "Kute, there is only so much sustenance I can provide you to aid in your healing."

"I am fine, Mother," Kute managed, grunting. He told Fabia about the piercing pain in his upper-left leg and the fact that he kept hearing Ygl in the room. She saw no wound, concluding Kute's experience stemmed from his connection to Ygl's jodepiece.

The nurses returned with the elixir, a fancy basket of herbs, and two doctors dressed in long robes and carrying baskets covered with cotton sheets. Fabia brought the elixir to Kute.

Erosc started crushing some of the herbs in his huge hands, allowing much of his fertility gift to stimulate the herbs' effects to the utmost. "This smell is intoxicating."

"That is a good thing, King Erosc," a doctor replied, producing a peculiar little knife.

Fabia elevated her son's head, holding the steel cup. "Drink the elixir, child. You will need it. Drink."

Kute grabbed her wrist, affirming, "I will heal."

"No," Fabia insisted, maintaining her composure. "You will not. You still bleed."

Erosc refused to pace. "Black magic is afoot. That spear was split in half by Man's divine right. Only Man controls magic, but this is darker because . . ."

Fabia knew Erosc refused to think his son would not heal because that meant Erosc himself would not heal, the bearer of every noble's divine right but hers.

Kute obeyed his mother's orders and drank the elixir.

The second doctor snapped a twig beneath Kute's nose, and he inhaled the fumes, causing him to get drowsy.

"I. Will. Heal," Kute affirmed.

"We will," the patient Fabia agreed, retaining tears. *Too much drama,* she thought to herself.

The herbal sap in Erosc's rough hands soon became a voluminous, sticky goo he dripped into a ten-inch bowl. "The ointment is ready, Doctors."

"Good," the doctor with the strange knife acknowledged.

"You know what must be done?" Erosc asked.

Two nurses went to place another cotton cushion under Kute's skull when they noticed Fabia's stern look. They relented.

Erosc resumed. "Fabia, you know what must be done."

"I know." She lifted Kute's head higher. "Discontinue your rhetoric."

"Is the scalpel ready?" the first surgeon asked.

"Of course," his coworker replied.

Fabia watched the scalpel slice down her son's abdomen for a midline incision near the fatal weapon. She and Erosc were quite familiar with surgical procedures and had known of Kute's rare injuries from past tourneys. Even rarer, their witnessing an impaling.

She was familiar with the surgeons' incisional probe into patients' bodies—the clean cloths soaking up the escaping blood, the gooey herbal ointment stopping the bleeding—but this should have never happened to Kute, the next heir to the estate with the divine right to heal as a secondary gift.

From the doctors, the parents learned that the ointment worked from the body's surface to block the bleeding while the elixir helped from within the blood. The surgeons' meticulous method was meant to ensure no internal damage while procuring the weapon and to maintain what the doctors called "hemostasis." For such a severe wound, all praise needed to go to Pyty, their goddess of the grains.

A nurse nudged Fabia's hand. "I am sorry, Queen Fabia. The king would like to converse with you."

Fabia noticed her husband just outside the doorway. He needed no gesture to motion her to join him in the adjacent hall. His demanding stare was enough. She allowed the nurse to hold Kute's head.

"I am going back into the battlefield," Erosc whispered once they convened in halls crawling with vibrant creepers garlanded with luscious fibers dripping crisp fruits and vegetables and lined with iron torches. "It seems everything is going fine."

"You are going to leave now?" She denied herself the fear of losing him while their son lay fighting for life.

"Kute must be avenged. That was a treacherous act upon him, and I will not allow it to go unpunished."

"Forgive me, Erosc, but we still have Umbala and Dionjor. I love Kute as much as you. We must be pragmatic." Fabia deemed herself as much a realist as Juna.

"You know Kute was always my favorite. And I will not have Sifya—"

"Umbala," she corrected him. She would defend their trans-son to the end.

He refused to correct himself. "This was magic at play here, Fabia. Magic. A spear was split in an attempt to assassinate me. A white smoke exuded from that split—"

"Maybe the Ogres—"

"No, this was no gift of their Divinity. We know the Ogres cannot control metals. Dwarves do. The god Xurchon is real. He must be stopped, and I will use everything in my power to stop him. Magic split that spear. Magic tried to make me meet the end. There is no way Man's divine right reaches this far.

"It is unfortunate, though. I failed to see the trickery until now. We all did, but to war we must go against the Ogres, and when we win—and we will—I will get to the bottom of this."

"And the Ogrean princess?" Fabia queried.

"I trust Kute. If he says she is good, I believe him."

"If you go into battle, she must fight beside you."

"That goes without saying. She is already out there." He peered over Fabia's shoulder. A tall figure in hoary armor approached from up the hall. Alduur. "What is he doing here?"

"Alduur is Kute's shield bearer, or has age diminished your memory?"

Erosc approached the former duke of the Northern Plantation, his former best friend, studying him. "I guess your pacifism works best here."

"Your son needs more than his parents by his side," Alduur replied with elegance beyond reproach.

"Do you demean me, shield bearer?" Erosc challenged.

Fabia intervened. "Let Alduur watch over Kute. He will be great company for me. For both of us."

Fabia studied her husband's earnest face, the desperation and fear in his blue eyes, the need for vengeance. The need to gather all the power he could. She touched his cheek with tender, supple fingertips. "I impart some of my divine right to you." Four of her tips rubbed softly. She could feel her vibrancy creeping into him, much like the luscious creepers in the halls, enticing him with supplemental energy. "You will need it."

She understood well the depth of the Elvin general's warning. Xurchon was a formidable foe, according to legend. And if he was real, then the Divinity had to be, too, and they needed to receive as much reverence as possible. "I wish I could be out there fighting alongside you with Kor'al, waving my sickle-lance high and proud."

Erosc smirked. "You are my spouse, my queen, and there is no other place I would rather you be. Our public needs you here."

"I know." She leaned in, pecking his cheek, imparting more of her infinite vitality. "Glory to Lolung-Cor," she whispered.

"Glory to Pyty," he replied, retreating down the hall teeming with fruity aromas and herbal scents and lined with iron-cast torches.

The tangy scent of jumbling bananas reminded Fabia of the clusters in Kute's bedroom hanging like chandeliers. Why her son would own so many bewildered her.

Erosc's bejeweled hair and beard tinkled and glistened with every stride. "Those foolish barbarians. They think they can dupe us about Kute owning their club. We would never dare visit them. Somebody must have snuck in and left it to him. They will rue the day they tried fooling us. They will rue."

The Giantic queen watched him depart and knew her choice of their "new son," Umbala, and Dionjor over Kute would not shock Erosc much. She was, after all, more pragmatic. Or was she? Did Erosc's desire for war and vengeance carry more weight than her hidden plea for no more loss?

She would miss Kute. Yes, she would, but her kingdom still had an heir.

"Shadocoat!" Erosc's deep voice bellowed with authority, his braids rattling against mirrored armor. He strode near the adjacent hall's terminus amongst the fruity creepers. She could hear his richness. "Shadocoat! Prepare my steed!"

Drama. Too much drama.

Alduur entered the operating room a bit nervously.

The procedure was ongoing; the bloodied weapon lay upon a nearby table. The surgeons worked feverishly to sew as much torn tissue as possible. The nurse slid a down-feather pillow under the unconscious prince's head.

The healing ointment and elixir were working well, but there was still so . . . much . . . blood.

Too much blood.

Alduur could not handle what he was witnessing, seeing his secret love a huge lump lying sideways. A lengthy tear lined Kute's massive back where the spear's point had exited.

"Suture. More suture," a calm surgeon ordered from the anterior. A nurse obliged, handing him another needle with a lengthy string attached.

Alduur shuddered. How he wished he could take back his words when he rejected Kute. His misplaced jealousy over Kute's privilege occluded his righteous anger when he led the LGBT parade against an unfair Erosc administration.

Yes, the former duke understood that Kute only wanted to protect him when the prince outed himself to a vengeful Erosc, who wanted to kill the defiant Alduur. Love made a Giant perform courageous acts.

The younger generation might instill in this older gent a thing or two. Maybe Alduur wanted to die a martyr after spending so long defying Erosc in the Northern Plantation, trying to make their kingdom greater than it already was in the Cories.

Alduur, the Duke of Denial. Maybe he was more ignorant than altruistic Kute.

A queasiness overtook Alduur. He sidled a little away from the bloody scene, closer to a promium counter. Promium, the hardiest metal alloy created by Dwarves. The blood bore too much of an effect on him. His own blood rushed to his head. He thudded against the wall.

He had made the wrong decision by coming in.

Alduur found himself slouched in the corner where the promium counter met the earthen wall. He must have fainted from all the blood, believing his selfless lover would not survive the disastrous affair. *Kute always found the good in everyone.*

When Alduur fainted, he had a dream—a "memorial awakening," Ygl would have called it. In the awakening, warm winds swept past Alduur's face, and his broad floppy hat was stuffed deep in a side satchel as he rode Powder's bleached wings through the cumulus clouds.

His pegasus raced its master over the haunting Dark Plains, Powder's hide obscuring Alduur's hoary armor well.

The Forest of Khun zipped along to the west. Alduur had planned to acquire lilies that tasted like sugar from there for his plantation before Erosc stripped him of his title.

But today, Alduur's thoughts lay elsewhere.

"Are you OK, Duke of the Northern Plantation?" the nurse whispered, leaning in to assist him.

"I am . . . Prince Kute's shield bearer." He objected, trying to deny his forsaken title, finally accepting his demotion to a position he had fought hard to protect those LGBT who wanted the option to remain warriors from.

"No." She smiled kindly, helping him up. "You will always be our duke." She presented him her linen sleeve. "We learned this from the Ogrean princess." She pulled her sleeve, revealing a kaleidoscopic tattoo of smashed fruits and vegetables, representing the LGBT flag Alduur bore in the parade. "Our duke," the nurse whispered in encouragement.

"Sutures," the surgeon ordered.

She ran to assist with the operation.

Chapter 14: The Uninvited

Somewhere in a mountain
Late-spring night/early morning

The deep cave's bleakness could not mask the obsidian luster of Swen's gases as she appeared in mid-space.

"General? Master Ygl, where are thee?" Her dismembered parts shifted, searching throughout the interior. *Oh, please don't make this such a mystery.* Her cosmic eyebrows furrowed over her vacuous eyes and pursing lips. "I heard thee call. I felt thy fear. I hope thou are somewhere near."

Her body parts continued flitting about, searching high and low, but could not find or even sense him.

She detected danger nearby. "Master Ygl, where did thou fall? Answer my call." Where her hairline should have been, starlight gases dispersed with every movement.

One of the floating runes in Swen's bodice— a hood with a bowl-shaped scoop below, a dot on both sides, and a medial line slashing through it— tingled strongly. Unknown danger approached. And with it, a strange sound. Was the mist approaching? The Death Mist? Her connection to Ygl called out to something, a reason to leave her sentry of the pegasi and her lamp's luxury. It has to be Demons stalking nearby. But within a mountain? Didn't Demons fear mountains?

Ygl & the Dwarf

She couldn't return to her Couch of Omniscience to attain knowledge of this eerie danger. Master Ygl was the priority.

"Master Ygl, where did thou fall?"

The danger approached too close, too fast. Swen stopped searching after hearing a humming sound, like bees buzzing.

She chanted with her tingling runes: "I spread my gases far and wide, from side to side, for the mist I must resist; on this, I insist. To be one with the spreading of the sun."

Like a web, the genie's nebulous form expanded. Her basic need: to protect her master.

Her hooded rune tingled stronger.

She glimpsed her foe, the lengthened shaft with engraved runes startling her, but even as she became familiar with the flying blade, her foe sped at her too fast.

The heavy hilt with the W-shaped cross guard alarmed her.

The auburn flame exploding around the sword dismayed her.

The humming. Swen recognized the humming.

"Welbern! Demonslayer! I'm not your taker!"

She began to chant again, her runes chiming more fiercely, but the sentient sword tore through her shifting form. Welbern's auburn flame crept across her celestial being in an irregular pattern, minimizing upon its exit, scattering her runes within her nebula.

Within the impact's flash, the genie found herself transported into the hellish Interim's dimension. The realm almost sucked her into a graying, smoky sea brimming with wailing residents.

A psychedelic sun roamed in the distance from this realm of unflappable magicks challenging hers.

To her astonishment, the Interim wouldn't take her. The eeriness seemed to change its mind. Despite this, Swen struggled against the dimensional power as if drowning in an ocean of sweet-and-sour bitterness.

The Interim expelled her. The portal closed.

An audible cackle seethed through her silent scream. Frightened, Swen turned to face her adversary as her stymied gases yearned to expand and blend.

Welbern departed. Ygl's broadsword disappeared into the darkness from which it came, perhaps searching for its master as well.

With a huff and a puff, the genie continued her webby transformation against a common foe.

Chapter 15: Patina

An incensed grogginess shook me from my slumber, another memorial awakening persisting.

This awakening made my enigmatic Khunian appear again. I had this same dream before the Dicen's attack at the Mous Strait near the Giantic Kingdom. The bloodied Khunian female postured, battle-ready, in her turquoise robe beside a roaring fireplace in a mysterious room, the fervor in her large eyes and gritted teeth matching the nearby flames, reeking of purpose.

Where was she?

"The children and I will not let this happen—" she challenged in her distinct Elvin accent.

Her opponent's silhouette loomed over her short stature, almost shrouding her pale skin.

The Khunian wielded Welbern with such resolve.

But this awakening proved a bit different. She spoke of children. She had children.

So frustrating! All these stupid awakenings with this and that tree creature, Tungloc, and I still had not gotten anywhere. Rondo and Xurchon's Death Mist still found me, all because of Ding's betrayal. Yeah, Kute tried reminding me about Ding being a thief, but Kute would know about this betrayal.

And what about the rest of the Party of the Jode? I had to maintain my control over their protection to keep them hidden from Xurchon. Ding might hold my piece, but I still held certain control.

All I knew was that we were losing. The Giants and Ogres had probably slaughtered each other, leaving Man to approach north and south to conquer the rest with their mist.

Horrible. Just horrible. What was the purpose of trying to get the Nixies as allies? It would be too late.

A peculiar azure radiance enveloped me in its icy light. Absent yellow tinges, I knew the radiance could not have been Ding finding an unearthly way to control my jodepiece.

Why would he join with the God of Evil? He was an atheist, my Achal. After all we had been through. I could only pray for him and everyone.

Pray. Me, pray?

Pounding my fists and crying were not getting me anywhere.

Limbus, my son, you are all that is left of my legacy. Be safe.

The azure light felt nice to me in the gloom. Where was I? Where was the light coming from? This had to be that same shifting light. I needed nourishment for my returning strength.

A shuffling behind me—and I had no weapon!

I gathered my mental energy, thrusting a psionic blast behind me before leaping into a roll, twisting to face my visitor, who yelped a lot.

My mind pictured a searing axe expelling metallic droplets, liquid fire, and . . . liquid earth?

I vaulted to the side as the red-hot axe crashed to the ground next to me, forcing me to cast a telekinetic armor about me. A tele-shield bloomed before me, blocking the weapon's next assault. Liquid metal and molten dirt splattered everywhere as I staggered.

Fifteen feet from me, an older Dwarven male stood with a curvaceous female picking herself up from the ground. Formfitting armor draped them with thick, furry tufts encircling their shoulders and waists.

"Nolly gee!" She appeared to be Kute's age, twenty-five.

"Are you all right, Patina?" the wheezing older male asked, sounding like he had inhaled too much of Inner Earth's bowels.

"I am fine, Pops." She brushed the dust off her chain-mail skirt. How odd. She did not wear a breastplate; instead, she wore a silver armored vest over what appeared to be a golden chain-mail shirt—*oh, she wore a tunic.* It seemed the Dwarves were just as fashionable as the Giants. How odd, indeed. Her vest had an emblem over her left chest: an apparent winged beast with a tail.

"This creature packs quite a mental wallop. Be careful. Nolly gee."

"I am," the commanding male confirmed.

My Achal! Blotches of liquid metal seeped from the male's pores, enveloping his exposed skin, encasing his graying goatee. He wielded his exquisite axe as part of his forearm—wait, the axe's handle was his forearm! I watched in amazement as the axe's head began splitting into five long, jagged daggers. A hand?

His hand! And similar to a Dicen's fanged fingers.

Smoky tassels swirled up from the divisions; earthen metal dribbled from the new creation.

My angry stare peered into the male Dwarf's wizened eyes, harboring much fear and anger, matching his newfound weapon.

"What manner of creature are you?" he asked. "You are not any manner of ditchightl we have encountered in the Epi-world."

"I am an Elf." I lurched down.

"An Elf?" He peered closer at me from his spot. "You look more like a Nixy."

The female peered more closely too. "Yeah, a Nixy." She chewed on a slender root.

I brushed myself off, maintaining some distance. "I have no idea what a Nixy is. I am an Elf from the Forest of Lorel."

"Lorel?" the inquisitive female echoed. I felt I might have a better rapport with her because of my psionic assault. She seemed more cautious and rational than her companion, but I needed to control my anger.

"Yes, miss," I answered. "Allow me to introduce myself to you. I am General Ygl of the Lorellians."

They paused for a moment.

"It is odd how it can speak to us. I must say quite politely, with some attitude," the female acknowledged, still rubbing her head.

"I say we kill it." The regal male's daggered fingers extended.

I frowned, thickening my telekinetic skin-shielding, the divine energy rising about two inches from my flesh.

The female grabbed the male's upper arm. "Please, Pops, let General Eagle of the Lorellians speak."

Ygl & the Dwarf

I did not need to read her mind to know she was naming me after the bird, but I get sick and tired of correcting people.

The stalwart male resisted until my infravision noticed his skin's fiery aura get a bit warmer. "Have at it," he submitted.

"Um, well, OK, Pops—"

Again, I drew his ire. He clenched his daggered fingers into a fist that fused into a huge hammer with a dagger pointing from its central axis. He raised his rigid weapon.

The earth trembled.

And I thought I had anger issues. I leaped back. "I do not have a moment to spare for your idiocy," I retorted. My infravision scanned about at the surrounding rocky wall's blue aura in the empty cavern, contrasting with Pops's fiery aura. There was really no place to run. My mind generated another psionic blast.

The female ran between us. She pleaded, "No, Pops. Do not do this."

Heat. Intense heat seemed to emanate from her. I increased my skin-shielding.

The earth trembled further.

A bizarre halo fizzled about her hands, liquid earth oozing out. The earth swirled around her hands like an amorphous ball of molten fire.

Pops hesitated. "Patina, move," he ordered.

"No," the calm Patina responded emphatically.

The reluctant male bit his inner lip. "Speak, Elf."

The female's portal shrunk; the trembles lessened.

My irritated words flowed with measure. "I have already spoken. I told you—"

"General Eagle of the Lorel Elves," the female interrupted. "I am—"

"Patina. Yes, I know. I guess you are a witch?"

"Me?" She started giggling.

"You seem to wield the heart of the twin suns."

More giggles surfaced around our threesome. My infravision scanned the area further, revealing more armor-wearing Dwarves with differing red auras.

She tried stifling her giggle. "A witch. No. More like Inner Earth's heart, nolly gee. A divine right from our goddess, Pariot. The sacred magma. I could assume the same of you." The amorphous ball of molten fire swirling about her hands subsided into a wispy halo encompassing the fiery portals.

As her ball simmered down, so did I. "I am not a witch, Patina. My gift has been granted to me by Achal, my goddess of history."

"Oh my . . ."

"He is the same as Ilinor," Pops muttered.

"Yes," Patina agreed.

Pops stared at me further, waiting for an answer.

"I was chased by Demons"—I regarded my outfit's tears—"much like the ones I am sure attacked your estate. A mist—a Death Mist, as it is called—harbors them. I fought them off with all my divine rights: telepathy, telekinesis, and precognition."

Mumbling replaced the sweet giggles.

"So many gifts," Pops replied. "Only the highest of royalty can be imparted such power."

Stunned, I thought for a moment. What this powerful Dwarf stated rang true. The thought of losing Methelo, Rolando, and Sylvia hurt so much to comprehend that attaining their divine rights became another issue I did not want to comprehend.

Yet with reluctant tears, I responded. "Yes. That would make me the king of the Lorel Elves. My family was murdered by Man. My kin have become enslaved by Man."

The mumbles grew.

"Kin?" Patina asked.

"Like 'people.'"

"Oh," Patina replied, "your kin have been enslaved, as have our folks."

"I know." I nodded, noticing I still retained a bit of my dialect.

"You knew?" Pops questioned. "From where you sit, we know you have never been within our estate."

"I am a member of the Party of the Jode. We were formed because we know the source behind your Demonic invasion is the Jode, or at least a piece of it, being wielded by Quirm's emperor, who, in turn, has been influenced by Xurchon."

The pair looked at each other, perplexed. The crowd mumbled further.

"Silence!" Pops ordered with a scowl. He turned to me, skeptical. "How do we know you are telling the truth?"

"Well, I guess you would have killed me when you had the chance. Here, let me raise the trust level." I stripped away my shielding's remnants. "See. Now I am vulnerable to you."

Approving, Patina diminished the rest of her divine right, her fiery portals whisking away in tasseled plumes. Her cautious face became clearer as she stepped forth, cute in a cherubic kind of way and dirty from hiding deep in these caverns for who knew how long.

"Patina," Pops warned. His stern tone expressed enough.

She hesitated. Her pouty lips puffed as she examined me closer. She positioned herself beside Pops's cool luminance to expose me better. Her slight smile gave her away. "An Elf, you say, eh?" Her question could not hide her excitement.

"Yes, Patina. I am an Elf. A Lorellian Elf and my kin's new leader since my family's unfortunate demise at Quirm. My kin have been enslaved, as I know yours have. And I take it, since you are not a witch, you must be a princess—and the fellow behind you a king?"

Her shapely lips parted a bit more. "Nolly gee," she murmured.

"Answer him, you fossil," an angry heckler yelled.

"Yes, he is the king of our realm," another answered.

"Silence." Pops did not hide his anger, making me wonder how I could best lessen mine in a similar situation. "Yes, King Eagle. I am King Qualt."

"And a mighty fine one he turned out to be," a female heckler criticized from the shadows. "He is the reason we are in the predicament we are in."

A male critic supported her. "Our lives will never be the same."

"Silence!" Qualt ordered again.

The very earth began to shake, trembling more than when Patina used her gift. Intense heat emanated from Qualt's form. His enhanced light-blue luminance forced the exposed crowd to cower. Their revealed faces appeared not fresh and healthy, like those of Qualt and his curvaceous princess. No, their faces were worn and ruddy, as if tired from many years of hard work. The crowd looked so much like . . . Ding.

I flung my kinetic armor back up.

Liquid metal exploded everywhere. Irregular spikes erupted from Qualt's body armor.

"Pops. Stop it!" Patina pleaded.

Pops? Yes, "Pops" must mean "Dad."

The cave shook and shook, casting its soiled bowels on us. The screaming hecklers scattered.

A twenty-pound boulder crashed onto me. My armor held, reminding me to protect these Dwarven kin. They might not be mine, but they might as well have been. Despite how Ding had wronged me, he still stood by me for many days. I would stand by his Dwarves.

Why? Because Ding hated everything and everyone. Ding especially hated Man. He protected me when we were prisoners at Chrot. We fought together against the Death Mist at the Ogrean kingdom and when the beasts attacked in the Dark Plains. When we were attacked in the Giantic kingdom, he stepped up to defend the Party. Why would he want to hurt his only friend, Kute? No, there was meaning behind his madness.

My skin-shield reached out—this fascinating product of my psionic divine right—invisible energy pulling from my flesh and bones, crawling into the air, tugging me, lifting me, but too much energy was being spent. This war had taken its toll.

I fell. And fell hard.

I mustered what precognitive instinct I could, focusing on the most endangered groups. Pulverizing the boulders would not be a good idea because the result would cause more frenzy. A better alternative would be catching the cave's bowels in a telekinetic net and casting it aside.

How fascinating for me to use my newfound gifts so skillfully. No doubt, my training with the Khunian Elves assisted me well in this regard.

A stalagmite fell toward the friendly princess, like the encumbered cave had lost a jagged tooth.

"Patina!" I yelled.

"Princess!" others called.

"What have I done?" Qualt muttered.

Through the shouts' gaps, I heard a familiar humming. Demonslayer swooped down in a bursting cloud of amber flames. My telekinesis slowed the heavy stalagmite's descent. *"Welbern! Quickly. Destroy it!"* my telepathic order rang.

With quick swings, my embellished sword cast a pair of arched flames at my earthen burden, weakening it before slicing it through, pulverizing the rock.

I leaped in front of shocked Patina. The air hardened around us, particles attached, sewn together by psionic energy weaving a telekinetic shield protecting us from further harm.

Patina shuddered next to me. "Thank you, King Eagle."

"King?" What a strange title to give me, an ill-begotten one at that—much like "general." *I better get used to it.*

"Are you OK, Patina?" I asked.

"Yes."

My Elvin ears perked. Amid the yammering and howling, I detected a different sound, like repetitive puffs on a hollow reed.

Wa-wa.

"What is that?"

Patina perked up. "Wolves and toles. Our mounts."

"Wow. Toles? Are they making that sound?"

"Yes. And yes."

A smaller crowd gathered again, muttering hatred and fear with wolves in tow. A hundred feet above, under a probable two-hundred-foot craggy ceiling, reddish forms with ten-foot wings circled slowly.

Wa-wa. Wa-wa.

Dirty Qualt straightened himself, his armor's irregular points glistening in his powdery luminance. "Patina." He stood as immovable as the stalagmite. "My little trinket, I am so sorry."

"Nolly gee, Pops. Do not apologize. We are all under a lot of stress."

As everyone surrounded us, Qualt stood maybe six feet from me but appeared detached from the rest. So much power, yet so alone. I could picture Emperor Rondo in the Dwarven king's place— Rondo, with his unfounded fear of all races—yet this picture held a slight difference because the emperor retained his kin's love while the races remained indifferent. Rondo's loneliness derived from paranoia, whereas Qualt seemed immovable, inside out. Qualt just did not care.

Patina stepped forward. "Folks, please calm down. Pops did not mean to do what he did." Impressive. They listened to her. This princess held much sway compared to Princess Gravelp. Was she the Princess Prodigy? She sure could chew on a root.

I reached up. Welbern's hilt smacked comfortably within my grasp, causing quiet in the clamor. "Demonslayer, you found me." I patted the hilt lovingly.

"Demonslayer?" a Dwarf asked. "Is that the—?"

"Yes, it is." I beamed. "How do you know of my blade?"

Qualt interrupted. "Everyone knows about the mightiest sword ever forged."

"Except you, you fossil," another heckler retorted. "You did not forge it. We did! Of the Meso-world!"

Qualt rejoined, "It was by the will of the gods, Henc and Pariot, that such beauty was created."

"To the Interim with the Divinity!" another protester spat.

"Where were your gods, Qualt?" another asked. "Where were they when the Demons attacked?"

Patina intervened. "Please. Please, my fellow Endos and Mesos!"

I whipped Welbern out of its sheath and held my blade high, amber flames crackling. The crowd grew silent. "Please," I pleaded, trying to maintain my anger. "I do not mean to frighten you. I have come from so far, and there is no patience for such bickering. Look at Demonslayer. What do your legends say about it?"

Patina fidgeted. "Well, partly, it was granted to the Elves for a past good deed we cannot remember."

"Therefore, the bond between our two estates is far stronger than anyone has anticipated. How we survived all these years without communication is beyond me. Please. Please. I beg of you. Please see that three parts of the legends have come true before you. Giants and Nixies are not your only neighbors. Elves and Ogres are too. And yes, the vast empire of Man thrives in the north. And if Demons are here, it can only mean the God of Evil has returned. And if he is real, then our gods and goddesses are as well. I know. I have seen them."

"Whom have you seen, king of Elves?" Qualt asked.

"Ethnel, the Essence of Faerie. When I say 'Faerie,' I do not just mean the Fairies of the Giantic estate. I also mean Pixies, Sprites, and Gnomes who worship this deity. And yes, there are such things as these other Faerie. Right now, the Pixies and Ogres are warring with the Giants and Fairies. The Sprites war against Man with the Gnomes and the Khunian Elves. Can you not see this is all real?"

"Can Demonslayer destroy the enemy?" someone asked from the illuminated shadows.

"Welbern has only so much effect. This is why I need your help. My kingdom has been captured as well. We must stand together before all is lost."

"What can we do?" the Dwarven king asked.

I paused. "I do not know. We-we were not supposed to come here. We were—"

"That is not what I meant, King Eagle. Look at where we are at. Man is out there. Most of my estate has been captured, imprisoned, and maybe met their deaths, and by all probabilities, I may have been at fault for much of it." Proud Qualt shuddered in his grief; his gilded armor's irregular spikes dwindled.

A deeper quiet encompassed the crowd, laden with a certain weight. A faint telepathic sweep uncovered some Dwarves touched by his admission.

"Pops," Patina noted, her face softened, "you—no one—could have ever predicted any of this occurring."

"I am sorry, King Qualt. This is not the moment to place blame. Strategy is of the utmost importance. It is not plausible to sit still while evil's forces search for the Jode."

Qualt turned to his kin. "Please, hear me. King Eagle is correct. If we have any chance of saving the estate, let it be now."

The dirty crowd paused, their silence deafening.

Someone remarked, "We do not listen to you—"

"Then listen to me," Patina interrupted. "I have been to the Meso-world and the Endo-world. Have I not? Have I not been among the folks working and toiling by your side? Have I not reached out to you? Do I not get some allegiance?"

Astounding. What did these royals do to their kin? These kin simply abhorred their king. Astounding.

"We will listen to you, Princess Patina," someone else responded. Approving mutters followed.

Such leadership Patina commanded. It would be weird if Patina was the Princess Prodigy, but that would be wishful thinking.

"Thankful," Patina replied before whistling to the ceiling. King Qualt tweeted his own special whistle. Others followed as the grimy audience dispersed.

A gust of air and windy flurry battered me. Wolfish reddish images sauntered to us from deep shadows.

Above, the windy disturbance's source glided down—toles. Huge toles with their reedy *wa-wa* sounds.

I could not describe what the toles looked like. Maybe owls—they had huge, owl-like eyes. The largest toles landed by their respective royals. As

Patina's settled, a ratty tail lashed gently from beneath a tuft of silvery tail feathers. Ten-foot feathered wings looked similar to bat wings, reminding me of my Steadfast. At the wings' apex, webbed claws. Clear, scrutinizing pupils waded within blackish pools. Silvery black streaks radiated around murky eyes—*oh, that emblem on Patina's vest, it represents the toles!*

"Lo, Twilight," Patina greeted.

Staccato chirps greeted their masters from jeweled harnesses.

"Down, Bantam!" Qualt whistled. His tole flashed mahogany colors with a dancing yellow-brown radiance.

Wolves jumped from a few toles' spines, some better kept than Ding's Redfang. A black wolf sauntered to Patina while a creamy one rushed to the Dwarven king, trying to lick Qualt's face off.

"Lo, Equinox." Patina petted her mount.

"Down, Icon!" Qualt ordered, flustered.

"Would you like to ride Twilight with me, King Eagle?" Patina inquired.

"I would be delighted, Princess."

Patina blew on a conch shell she pulled off Twilight's harness, disturbing my sensitive hearing. Her conch shell was different from the Giants', with a metallic mouthpiece and a cylinder encircling the bell's interior. Patina's finger pushed a small button, allowing her to use her horn much like Mitral's echoing booms. "Folks, please listen, my messengers on wing. Tell the others to meet at the Northern Forge. We need to strategize."

Fascinating. Dwarves were designers like the Giants and Fairies, but a different kind of designer. "You are having everyone go?" I asked. My eyebrows had yet to lower from the fascination.

"Why not? The Demons will not travel this far."

"OK, but Man will not hesitate because of the distance."

Patina paused for a fleeting thought. She smiled. "My king, we cannot take the general out of you. Very good." With a "nolly gee" and the pressing of pouty lips on metal mouthpiece, she redirected her supporters. Apparently, the Meso-world had many entryways.

My dead brother, King Methelo, was nothing like me. He cared more about being a diplomat than learning the art of battle. To this degree, Methelo did not differ from Emperor Rondo, and that behavior may have been Methelo's undoing, leading to our kin's demise. Oh, Methelo . . .

I moved myself in front of Patina, nestling near Equinox's hindquarters. Patina kicked Twilight's sides and whistled. The great silvery tole spread tapered wings, bounced along the ground a little, and soared into the blackened air. The launch was not as graceful as my Steadfast would have performed, but the silence of Twilight's flapping amazed me.

"Now we can stop Ding from doing anything foolish," I muttered.

Patina hesitated. "What did you say, Eagle?"

"Ding. Ding is the Dwarven thief who was with my party. He stole my jodepiece from me when we entered this cave. He is an idiot because even I had a difficult task controlling it, even with my telepathy. We have to stop him."

"Your te-le—"

"Telepathy. *Telepathy*."

Patina jolted. "Oh, this is how you struck my mind."

"Yes. And I apologize for that."

"That is OK. Can you speak to me in that manner? I would like to know more about your journey with this Ding."

I felt a mystic tugging trying to pull me into a more southwestern direction. *"Of course."*

Chapter 16: The Giantic-Ogrean War

The pasture between the Cory Mountains
and Dark Plains
Morning's breaking dawn

The rain slashed like knives.

The winds attempted to slice skin apart.

The twin suns' corona tried to break through the storming thunderheads.

Queen Juna locked onto her divine rights' source as if her Fairy public focused through her. The intent, so strong.

She connected with the winds so well, her fluorescent wings melded with the chaotic molecules, disappearing into them—the airy chaos transforming into new wings. Her body, her skin more porous, almost scattering with the blustery mayhem beyond her comprehension.

Watery Gasma, on the other hand, had absorbed so much moisture, her Pixy size stretched to greater heights and lengths—a swirling epitome of aquatic turbulence.

The queens' elemental convergence became unbearable for the armies.

Even Juna's husband, Ood, wielder of the black light, retreated quickly, like the Pixy Council.

"You cannot hope to defeat me, mud licker," jeered Gasma.

"Try me, sand sucker!" Juna whistled.

Ygl & the Dwarf

Juna's connection to air and light had become so strong, she could sense beneath the descent of Gasma's aquatic toes the massive armies' attempt to battle on. The battering weather, a grandiose wave of disorder, edged inward, taking a taxing toll. Like a sledgehammer, a windy gust pounded a gaggle of Giants and Ogres into the sky like a bushel of leaves.

Juna gasped at how chaotic her divine right had become; seeing her allies being assaulted, she pressed on.

Her divine right slammed hard into Gasma's with a torrential temper, the very sky eaten alive with celestial passion. Air and water. Wind and rain. The ingredients of a hurricane.

Pegasi and gryphons alike initiated an evasion to their respective camps. Even Fairy and Pixy evaded, being bowled over like flies.

The only aerial mounts that remained locked in fatal combat were aquiline Pillager and reddish Slab. The gryphon and pegasus stayed because their masters performed the same dance below.

General Umbala's face-off with General Punok became a struggle with the piling hurricane. He sheltered behind his hefty shield, unable to exploit his opponent's divine right, his immense strength providing him firm footing as their trudging toward each other continued.

"Blast this storm!" Giantic Umbala gritted his teeth, keeping his sickle-lance near as he edged closer to the dark-skinned Ogre.

He could see that Punok's increased mass withstood the hurricane flurry's strength to a maximum.

The Ogre shoved his chisel-spear deep into the ground, anchoring himself closer and closer to burly Umbala. Punok's ebon face half-masked behind his chimaera cloak's sleeve.

True. Never had anyone felt weather like this. Dirt and rock, whirling daggers. Uprooted grasses.

Umbala witnessed Gasma and Juna performing their torrential dance, their cosmic ballet, despite the tempest's blur. Juna spiraled through Gasma, trying to attack from the side, but Gasma caught her. The desperate queens entwined—flood and gales colliding—higher and higher toward the thundering nimbus.

Their forms transformed, more transcendent with every twist.

Chapter 17: Quirm

Gablen, the capital
Morning's breaking dawn

"I don't understand what's going on," Emperor Rondo said, frustrated, trying to study the mystic map of Zaendara glowing in the ten feet between Xurchon and himself. He glanced about his dimmed throne room, and pale vapors anguished. The empty five thrones, not far away.

"Calm down." Xurchon's firm voice was sweet as apricots; his waxen smoke obscured his athletic build's nakedness.

"Calm down? My lord, that's what I'm trying to do, but I don't understand this. First, I see a favorable war, and now I see this. What's going on?"

The God of Evil, appearing like the purest teenage boy, just stared at Man's emperor sweetly.

"My lord, please," Rondo pleaded, focusing on the pasture between the Cory Mountains and the Dark Plains. "All I see is this powerful storm pushing the two forces apart while two other forces fight from within."

With a slight gesture of his sinewy arm, Xurchon allowed the minuscule scene to shift and surge upon itself, ballooning to a more definite picture beaming between the two attendees.

"What is this?" Quirm's emperor asked.

"It's what thou asked for, Rondo. The two queens are fighting each other."

"I do not understand. What's this huge water woman?" the frustrated Rondo queried.

"A Pixy queen. That is Gasma battling Queen Juna."

"But where?"

"Juna is hidden somewhere in that cyclonic mess that keeps attacking Gasma."

"How? How are they able to survive this?"

"Because they control a power unbridled."

"They alone can survive this? They're so small . . . with so much power. Is this something we should—?"

"Of course not."

"But, Xurchon—"

"They're of no concern. We'll win. Just wait. My Raaligor are taming your insurgents."

Rondo gawked at them, feeling an unraveling buildup within, ignoring his god's last statement. He reached out to the map. "I could crush them. Could I not?"

"I'd advise you not to do so."

The lightning flashes licking the battleground awed Rondo. Who could withstand this? How could he win?

Xurchon continued. "There's power that sleeps. Let it sleep."

Rondo watched the lightning tear into the evading armies, remembering his accidental psionic incident with his jodepiece when he attended to Sama some days ago. "You know more than I."

Indeed, Xurchon wished he knew more, for he couldn't understand how his enchanted spears had disappeared. The spears meant to kill Giantic King Erosc had suddenly vanished before reaching the surviving king. Stronger power played here. Strong enough to defy even him. Ygl's jodepiece could accomplish such a feat, and where the piece hid, Xurchon knew the Lorellian general idled nearby.

But where?

Xurchon's omniscience did not need the mystic map when he beheld the mounted Giantic king turning on his sable pegasus when the chisel-spears disappeared behind him. Could King Erosc be harboring the jodepiece? No, very few had the capability to tolerate such power. No, this General Ygl must be near.

Xurchon's omniscience also found it difficult to understand King Erosc's strange behavior before the armies charged across the field to engage in battle. Where did the Giantic king disappear to once he swept his arm to the ground? Well, the answer came in Erosc's sable pegasus returning to the Cory Mountains and appearing in the stalls and Erosc appearing in a surgery room, looking at something that was nothing. The surgeons were working on something, but he couldn't see it. A strange ritual, indeed.

Xurchon's suspicions grew when he heard his name being called. The source: that pudgy Dwarven thief in a cave. How did the thief get there? The dirty Dwarf screamed about something being in the cave, but the God of Evil couldn't confirm.

Nonetheless, Rondo sent his mist through his piece's portal in hopes of capturing the elusive General Ygl. If the Dwarf was there, so was that dratted Elf. To Xurchon's satisfied amazement, the Elvin general let his cloaked presence be known through his sword Welbern's reaped slaughters charring with auburn flames, yet both remained unseen.

Ygl's jodepiece was truly a powerful artifact. All the more reason Xurchon needed to have the gem as a whole. Somehow, Ygl was able to utilize his piece to cloak the Party and himself.

Despite the Death Mist's protection, his Demons still feared the mountains' historical hidden power. The Demons couldn't confirm Ygl but knew many of their own died in the pursuit.

Xurchon felt the mountains' protective energy at first when his omniscience witnessed an unknown force slaughtering the Dark Plains denizen. Later, his Cindiru shrieked another inaudible warning before being stripped away from the Giantic advisor's body and killed.

Xurchon sensed Demonslayer's distinct kiss at that point, revealing to him what his Cindiru could see that he couldn't. The only power greater than Xurchon was the Jode, and only one person wielded the Seeker of Souls, Welbern, the Demonslayer.

No doubt. The God of Evil had an idea where Ygl, Kute, and Juna hid. But where were Swen, the genie, and Princess Gravelp of the Ogres?

A rapid rapping thudded upon the hidden walls.

Darkness's slivers enveloped Xurchon.

"Open," Rondo commanded after Xurchon had camouflaged himself. The appearance of a door's silhouette swirled with the pale vapors; bluish-yellow spangles split the whirling convergence.

A meek messenger hurried through. "M-my emperor, we have need of your word. The Lorellian slaves have become too rebellious. Many citizens are worried they may have gotten the message of Khun's resistance. What should we do?"

"You know what to do, Rondo," Xurchon encouraged.

Rondo hated what he had to do next. These Lorellians had become too emboldened. He had committed so much in the name of love. Why could they not understand he was more than they could ever believe?

More extreme measures were needed.

Rondo turned to his messenger. "I want the males separated from the females and children and detained in the cities—the major cities—including Vante and Wyp—"

"Excuse me, Emperor," the meek messenger interrupted.

"Yes?" Rondo replied, a slight frown creasing his grave face.

"De-detained in what?"

"Camps. The children. Kill the children first."

Distraught, Sama the Nixy sought out Rondo's throne room in the secluded hall few traveled. She needed to tell her trusted guardian about her lost child, to speak more to him about his children. His missing children, like her missing Ryl. She needed to tell him about Tungloc, the dendruid who could help them find Ryl and maybe find his children.

She needed to speak to him about the humads, the hydroyids, and the aether. So much to talk about. She needed to tell him about the Nameless. Yes, that was their name. The Nameless.

A seven-foot guard blocked her path.

Smoke appeared below Rondo's large oaken doors—no, a mist. A mist with bluish-yellow spangles!

"No," Sama muttered, fearing for Rondo's life.

Another guard blocked her advance again.

Taken aback, Sama examined the stalwart guards. Maybe it was because Rondo's illusion spell cloaked her to look like a blonde Quirmean that they didn't notice her true Nixy form.

Wait. The mist that attacked her son and her in the Forest of Lorel had flaunted the same bluish-yellow spangles.

Sama performed her best effort at calmness, backing away, realizing the certainty behind her Quirmean benefactor being unlike Tungloc, the dendruid. Rondo, after all, wielded the same bluish-yellow spangles.

Why hadn't she figured this out before? The mist and Rondo were the same. *He is the reason behind my Ryl's misfortune.*

She'd need to make new plans.

* * *

Hethomes College of Academics
Vante, Northern Quirm

Ygl left Captain Lyp to spearhead the Lorellian rebellion before escaping Chrot. The sixty-year-old hadn't expected the rebellion to progress so well because he hadn't expected so many Quirmeans to be against their emperor's endeavor. Still, Quirm was a vast empire where the majority ruled.

He claimed he tried to save Ygl from certain death at Skavir's Torture House, but he misspoke and remained grateful for Ygl making the sacrifice to replace his wife and himself, sending them to the slave city of Chrot instead. Lyp became more impressed with his general's courage in saving the Dwarf and the Giant who were Chrotian prisoners with them. General Ygl never ceased to amaze Lyp.

Ygl & the Dwarf

"No more war! No more war!" The college students' protest had gone on for days at the campus named after their emperor's mother. At first, many students remained quiet about Emperor Rondo's war. Until they heard about their beloved campus being turned into a detention camp. Until they heard about the rebellion.

Not the Elves' rebellion—other Quirmeans themselves. Lyp understood the Quirmeans became emboldened upon hearing about Princess Jonas's endeavors in the Forest of Lorel, gladdened to know someone in the royal family retained some sanity.

Captain Lyp agreed with them. How could the emperor do this? Quirm had a thriving economy. Why would he attack sovereign estates? And now, he wanted to make their scholastic city into a camp. A detention camp. Madness!

Lyp helped organize the student body's massive numbers. Too massive. Quirmean soldiers couldn't contain them. When the soldiers thought they had a faction contained, students would throw hard items from nearby windows, cowing the soldiers.

The struggle stretched from the administration buildings to the sports fields to the academic halls to the dorms.

The southern bridge, with its sixty-foot tunnel, separated the dorms from city life. This late evening, an athletic star led the protesters to the tunnel. They were going to take their protests to the streets.

Lyp noticed the enigmatic athlete who led the campaign, a popular substitute for the sports captain who had somehow disappeared. But with this new captain, the Lorellian's infravision noticed a red aura

135

heavier than everyone else's. This new captain's body temperature was unnaturally higher.

Lyp tried to warn his coconspirators, but no one listened since the athlete had won awards for the college. That was all that mattered to them.

Elico. That's right. The new star's name was Elico.

"This way," Elico's voice tooted. He led an eager crowd of sixty down the tunnel, a quarter block wide.

Lyp stayed at the group's tail end, worried.

Strange. The tunnel was dark. Lyp's infravision caught sporadic spots of red aura along the wall—the torches were doused!

Lyp could see Elico's hand holding the only torch aloft in front, a hand whose red aura deepened, matching the torch's blaze.

The torch was heaved out the tunnel's other end. Elico turned, grinning, and he grew bigger, melding with the encroaching shadows, his red aura deeper than the torch's.

The tunnel became unbearably hot. Being in his midfifties, Lyp hurried out before fainting.

"Mortal fools. You belong to Elico the Huge. Remember the Raaligor when you journey to the bowels of my sire," Elico tooted with a hissing cackle. His hands, two feet thick, sprang from the dim surroundings.

Lyp dodged the monstrous, shadowy fingers, rolling beneath them, and escaped the tunnel's murk.

Too late for the others. The burning hands enveloped the protesters from every direction.

Screams—too many—poured from the tunnel's thick umbra. Blood flooded out as if driven by the screams, pushing the straggling protesters and Lyp back.

Lyp put on his hood and ran away. For sure, Xurchon was playing a stronger hand in this war, making this harder for everyone. *This is a disaster.*

Lyp remembered a dream he'd had. The dream seemed so real, almost like a memory returning. Ygl fought a pair of monsters called tridras while riding his unipegon, Steadfast. Lyp was forty-six then; the sixteen-year-old's captain. Ygl and he were able to kill the first tridra, and a tree creature called Tungloc killed the second. But that was it. Lyp could remember nothing else.

If anything mattered now, Lyp wished Ygl—or Tungloc, for that matter—would appear next to him to deal with this devastating Elico the Huge of the Raaligor.

In the following days, the southern gates were boarded, along with their three sister gates. Soldiers stood guard, quelling any more dissent.

Chapter 18: Limbus, Ygl's Son: Mission Possible

Chrot, slave city of Quirm

Limbus hid with Ploone in an alley in the dirty town with his asegafian cat, Snip. He observed the old and visiting slaves from between the beechen structures. The alley, rather narrow, was a perfect fit for them, with three crates acting as a wall behind them, a magnet for the scattered trash laziness refused to throw away.

Ploone's feline, Winky, lay next to Snip, the two resting from all their teleporting. Born in the same litter as Snip, Winky had fur lighter and less furry than Snip's.

Though asegafians didn't teleport long distances, their travels weren't short ones. Thus, teleporting around the extensive Wall of Quirm from the Forest of Khun to attempt espionage was not an easy task. The young Lorellians' favored pets needed to catch a breather under the evening's sky.

Khunian Chieftess Rungna had sent them in Chrot's easterly direction, advising that some birds had seen marching slaves.

Limbus found the angular city dreary even without the slaves. Livestock, with their musky smells, appeared to be bought and sold here, but Limbus focused on the main gate, so he couldn't see much from behind a wagon's wheel.

Ploone reported from the alley's other side that shops sold meals.

Meals? In a place being packed with Lorellian slaves? Well, people had to eat.

But the Lorellian slaves certainly weren't the ones being fed. Their gaunt frames frustrated Limbus. He even witnessed an Elf forced to beat a defiant one.

Oh, goddess Achal . . . something had to be done.

Limbus was glad the Khunian Elves' defense of their neighboring forest thwarted Quirm's advance—twice—adding to Quirmean anxiety, emboldening Limbus.

The chained slaves didn't shuffle single file through Chrot's main gate on the balding ground. Instead, they were amassed. Layer upon dusty layer stirred and swayed into the air as link upon link of chain rubbed against the dirt.

Something big had to be going on. Too many people amassed.

The marchers had much fear, but the occupied carts leaving the city concerned the marchers more. Fellow Lorellians of every age were compacted within the wooden bars. The bars at least provided their cargo with fresh air. The cargo's discomfort, the least concern.

"Where are they taking you?" a marching Elf yelled.

An elderly woman, weary from too many chores, stretched a bony arm between the bars. "To Skavir. They take us to Skavir," she croaked.

The marchers and Limbus gasped.

Skavir, home of the Torture House. Limbus remembered his dad telling him this when Ygl fought the manticora and saved Captain Lyp there.

He knew his people would never return from such a site, hope already a dim glimmer fading away.

"Did you hear that?" Ploone whispered.

"Of course I did. I'm right here." Limbus's lips pursed.

"We should go attack them," Ploone insisted, clenching his fists.

"Rungna and Blasmle said to observe the marchers."

"Come on, L. There are kids there. We didn't save them all. Who cares what Blasmle and Rungna say? We're saving those Lorellians."

"No. There are too many guards, and we have too few arrows. Winky and Snip need energy too."

"They've been resting all day," Ploone whined.

Day? Limbus wondered, so frustrated their dialect had disappeared. "Ploone, I love you, but every so often, I think you're more headstrong than me."

Ploone became more insistent. "L, those are Lorellians. They need us. All Rungna said was that birds saw marchers. OK, I see them, too, but I also see more kids we can save."

"Oh, to pee in the mouth of a lotus flycatcher." Limbus gave his bestie a glare. "What do you want me to do? Blasmle asked us to spy. We have others in our Children's Brigade checking other places."

"You know your dad wouldn't like you talking this way," Ploone reminded him.

Limbus paused in thought, embarrassed. "I think we should meet at the rendezvous point and discuss this. You're right, Ploone; we are Lorellians before we're anything else—even Khunians. My dad is sacrificing himself for us."

Ygl & the Dwarf

Limbus sat against the beech wall's peeling paint, petting Snip, who lapped vestiges from a rusty water bowl. Snip's bulbous mauve eyes blinked.

Limbus missed his dad sorely. He missed his family. His mom, Thalla, nurtured and coddled him. She even taught him independence in her own way. For instance, when Ygl went on tours, she taught Limbus how to deal with Ygl's absence, but when she left her only son alone in Lorel's bosom to search for berries, Limbus sensed she hid somewhere, observing him from behind a bush or on a branch.

With no one to watch over him now, Limbus felt different—vulnerable. Maybe Ploone would be the new replacement.

"Ploone, do you remember when Dad took me on trips to Quirm's capital, Gablen?"

"You mean to that castle you've 'barely been to' but just happened to have a specific memorial dream about?"

"Yes," Limbus answered, embarrassed.

"He took you to Khun too."

"Yeah. Gablen was diplomatic. I am not sure if it was him or Uncle Methelo, but they wanted to fix a supposed strained relationship between our estates. I remember something really bad happened, but I can't remember what. Something about a little boy or girl, I think."

"You think?" Ploone jested, keeping a lookout. "I know he had a lot of trust in you to take you there."

Limbus smiled. "Yeah. But the trips to Khun were more fun and frequent."

"He never wanted to let you out of his sight." Ploone giggled.

"No." Limbus paused in thought. "I wonder if he ever felt abandoned. I don't think our grandparents ever abandoned him, but he rarely spoke about them, especially our grandmother, Rarle. She could see the past.

"But he got along so well with Chief Blasmle and Chieftess Rungna of Khun. They showed us how to make and use weapons. Dad taught us how to use them, and they taught Dad."

"Yeah, but can we talk about this later?" Ploone kept an eye out for more guards. "We've got a much more pressing matter at hand."

"You don't think I know that? I'm the one who volunteered us for Rungna's mission against this crazy emperor."

"I know. I was there. You wouldn't take no for an answer from the chiefs."

"Because they wouldn't let us travel farther into Lorel with them. What can I say? I have Dad's stubbornness." Limbus hesitated. "I was there, you know."

"Where?" Ploone asked, mystified.

"When Dad and Uncle Methelo argued about protecting Lorel against Man's invasion during the spring dance. Dad wanted more troops. Methelo wouldn't give them. That's why I made the decision to gather our friends and as many kids as I could to escape on the asegafians. I wasn't going to wait to ask Dad."

"He probably would've agreed."

"And probably wouldn't, considering he didn't want to abandon me."

"Yep. You're stubborn," Ploone scoffed.

Limbus smirked at the compliment. He revered Ygl, happy to bear the mantle of "Little General" that Chieftess Rungna of the Khunian Elves bequeathed him when he saved her from being killed when her forces diverted Man's from the sacred forest. Limbus hoped to make Dad proud—maybe even Blasmle and her too.

He peeked around the corner beside Ploone, resting on all fours. "It's a lonely world," he whispered.

Ploone's thick hand rubbed Limbus's back. "You know I'm not going anywhere."

Limbus transfixed upon the clasping. "I know."

"You know how we're sounding more like them the more we stay in this stupid empire."

"Yeah, we're talking in what they call contractions. Are you ready to raise the Children's Brigade's ranks?"

Ploone smirked. "Of course."

They touched their cats and vanished.

Chapter 19: The Northern Forge

The Dwarf kingdom

Glassy jewels speckled the cool panoramic cavern with walls maybe one hundred feet high lined with five-foot platinum tiles. The forge glistened, unlike the more opaque stones at the Ogrean kingdom: opals, jades, agates, and such.

"Your forge is almost as beautiful as you, Patina," I commented innocently.

"Nolly gee." The modest princess grimaced, pulling another slender root from her vest's inner pocket. "I guess. It is certainly as wide as my hips." She chewed on the end.

"I am serious."

"Well, OK," she flirted. "Pretty does not come cheap, King." Her twang became more pronounced.

"Oh, I apologize. I did not mean to insinuate—"

She patted my shoulder. "No. I understand. You are still sweet on your Thalla."

In truth, Patina was correct. Yes, I missed my cherished Thalla, but Swen had filled my thoughts of late. My genie held such sway over me. A sway that surpassed her allure and the deepest of her incantations. My sentry with the steeds. I could call her but not yet.

Patina eyed the mesh netting running down my vest's left sleeve and my pants' grapevine design with a smirk. "You Lorel Elves seem fashionable."

"I got this from the Giants."

"Ha! I should have known." She laughed, snatching the root from her mouth. "No one but Giants."

I browsed around. Among the organized axes and hammers, scattered swords, shields, lances, and sickles added to the décor. A strange three-pronged weapon rested not too far away. Were some of these Quirmean? Each weapon, exquisite in shape and design. Without a doubt, much work was accomplished here. "This place is amazing. These items. What are they called?"

Qualt entered the conversation. "These are what we call our inventions. Besides accumulating wealth, Dwarves love to invent. The Northern Forge is the grandest of all the forges, King Eagle. We keep all our prized assets here, about two miles' worth. This is why it is kept heavily guarded."

"It amazes me you have all this weaponry for the entire continent."

"Yes. We made all this."

"You old fossil," heckled an old female in rags, her skin not as ruddy as Ding's, "you did not make anything. We did!"

The embattled Dwarven king did not respond as the crowd followed us. The wolves, Icon and Equinox, trotted on either side, protecting their masters with a squad of guards. The old heckler and some followers appeared quite pale, while others looked ruddy, like Ding. None of them had the perfectly tanned skin Qualt, Patina, and their guards exhibited.

"And not all of us share in the wealth," a ruddy follower retorted.

"As you can see, King Eagle—" Patina attempted to send to me.

"Please, just call me Ygl, Patina. I have not been crowned yet."

"OK. As you can see, our folks still have many issues with my pops."

"Are we sharing our link with your pops?"

"Of course." Patina giggled.

I maintained the psychic link with Qualt and her, making sure our link did not jolt his older mind.

I continued. *"I can see your people hate your dad, Patina, and I am sorry to hear it. They remind me of Ding. May I ask, are we here looking for something?"*

"Yes, we are, and we are almost there. I must tell you, I have found your adventures quite intriguing, especially about this Ding person. You said he had a wolf?"

"Yes. Redfang."

"Hmm . . ."

"What?"

Qualt intervened. *"I hear everything, my little trinket. I think we should tell the honorable king about the Ding we know."*

I welcomed their disclosure and found his nickname for Patina endearing. *"Please do."*

Qualt continued, adjusting his armor. *"The Ding we know was scheduled to be executed."*

I pretended not to know that bit of information. *"Wow. That is quite a load to lay on me. For what?"*

"Treason. The thief we know was an atheist and anarchist who wanted to overthrow our government."

Treason? Ding, that was quite a mess.

"Well, here we are." Patina interceded with a proud wave as we strolled around a diamond-strewn bend lined with iron braces. "This is what we feel Man may want from us."

Whatever was positioned before us, the device loomed, incredible to witness. Ten-foot wagon wheels forged of sturdy metal they called promium hoisted the woody behemoth. The wheels had spokes and connected to a sixty-foot rectangular base, maybe fifteen feet high.

A second level held two compartments. The rear compartment was five feet larger than the front, which stretched longer, with a thinner attachment sticking out like an odd branch. A few vertical, stemlike windows adorned most of the base and sides of the top compartments. The top rear compartment flaunted two-foot bilateral windows. Gold braces adorned all portals.

Qualt climbed up the monstrous wagon's ladder leading to the base's oaken door. He peered down at me. "You can come up, King Eagle. I am the only one who can control the spectral cannon right now . . . My trinket, you know there is room for you also."

"I thought you said Man would not come here?"

Patina blushed. "Well, in all honesty, nolly gee, we did not remember that entrance where the mist arrived. And the thought really slipped our minds. Oh, how I miss Ilinor."

"Who is he?" I asked.

"Our general," Patina answered. "Much like you before your ascendance. I miss Eifnor too. He was our doctor and advisor and taught me much."

"Where are they?"

"We do not know. We only know they are not with us."

We climbed into the spectral cannon's interior. I had to duck my head a bit. Patina called it a cabin, passing through the lengthier cabin below. From what I could ascertain, rows of seats aligned with adjacent poles sticking out from the walls close to the promium wheels. Did the Dwarves turn the poles to turn the wheels?

Where we arrived became more important to me because so many more poles, sticks, and buttons were scattered everywhere. Strange torch holders poked from the walls, maybe five feet in length, slit down the middle, the closer side somewhat lengthier than the opposing one.

I scanned the ceiling. Reflective glass—mirrors—climbed in staggered, inconsistent steps to a central opening. From that epicenter, something like a vertical wheel was propped beneath, exhibiting a single outcropping of holders on its perimeter. Within each of these holders, a different gem rested. At top, a possible ruby. "I cannot believe this. What does it do?"

King Qualt remained stoic.

"Nolly gee, it is probably best if I show you, Eagle." Patina leaned out the cabin's doorway, calling out to the crowd. "Could one of you folks please prop any item in front of the cannon?"

"Would the princess like for us to get into the cannon?" someone asked.

"No, thank you. The item will be sufficient." Patina winked.

As they communicated, Qualt turned the wheel. As the wheel rotated, the gem holders kept their individual caches in position. The wheel stopped with a dark purple jewel on top.

Patina ran inside to grab strange sticks attached upright to a circular wood pairing. From the pairing's center, a round chain shot up like a necklace, attaching to a central post and two other wooden circles. From that attachment, another chain necklace stretched into a frontal opening coated in metal.

"What are you doing, Patina?" I asked.

"I am turning gears to aim the cannon's barrel."

A coolness brushed my posterior as Qualt demonstrated his divine right's aspect, which balanced his body's molten forgery. Light-blue luminance danced on the walls.

Qualt perched behind me on a crude gilded throne of his making, the backing's top rail bathing in the brightness as the magma pouring from his being shaped the last touches to the finial on top. Behind his throne, a fifteen-foot steel crater emerged, maybe a sitting area within the wall. He straightened with pride.

"You are actually our first royal audience, King Eagle. Take this as quite an honor."

He extended an aged hand toward the purplish gem. With a spittering and sputtering, his liquid metal lurched upon layers of itself from his skin, over and past his hand, molding itself into a smaller version of the cannon's barrel, a voluminous bulb popping at the end, a pointy extension protruding from the bulb. "You may want to cover your eyes, King," he advised.

I tried, but curiosity forced me to peek through my fingers.

A portion of Qualt's luminance focused on his molten construct and flashed out from the bulb's endpoint into the purple jewel. From the jewel, a stronger beam erupted into the cannon's barrel.

"Go, Eagle," Qualt instructed. "Look out the windows."

Vertical windows like slender, curved dashes granted me another peek at the outside from the upper opening's area: a square shield propped against a boulder. The violet beam struck its center.

Ice formed on the spot. Ice!

Patina giggled. "Now watch this." She rotated a different set of gears.

The cannon's mouth expanded wider. The beam grew bigger, covering the entire shield and encasing the shield in more ice.

I gasped. "What manner of magic is this?"

Patina chuckled. "Magic this is not. This is what the Meso-Dwarves call 'Pariot's Knowledge.' Pariot is our goddess of invention and the wielder of the hammer of sacred magma. We do not know which counterbalances which, but it is certainly an interesting evolution. Do you not think?" She pulled a root from within her vest and chewed on the morsel's tip.

"Of . . . of course. I agree."

"This is what we think Man wants," her pops added. "The day Ding was to be executed in Zak, this mist appeared out of nowhere, harboring those Demons. As you know, it was impossible to fight back and to know who was captured or met death. We defended ourselves as best we could, but this foul mist seemed to swallow even our divine rights. By the sacred magma, we lost Ilinor and Eifnor. Everything seemed hopeless. Our only way to escape was the mountains behind us, but Quirm's army emerged, trying to block our path. We knew we had to help the Mesos and Endos escape, but with waning powers . . ."

Ygl & the Dwarf

The proud Dwarf's silence, heart-wrenching. He whimpered.

Patina hugged her pops. He grew rigid and tried hiding his face.

She continued for him. "With the mist behind us and Quirm's army blocking us, we were corralled. No one expected this attack. Who knew, nolly gee? We thought we were at peace. Certainly, the warring Giants never bothered to attack us. We were good business for them. My pops and I prepared ourselves for capture, and then it happened."

"What?" I asked.

"Well, this." She motioned to Qualt. "Pops?"

Qualt's re-formed hand grabbed his bubbly daughter's soft palm. He kept his proud head down, away from prying eyes. The moment they clasped, they levitated off the ground.

Confusion settled in me. "You can fly. Is this not one of your gifts?"

Grim Qualt answered, "No, it is not. This is what has confounded us."

"Unlike the Giants, whom we believe are much warmer toward each other than our folks, Dwarves are not as—shall I say—touchy-feely with our emotions. We certainly do not hold hands."

Something pulled at me from my gut; an unearthly tugging latched onto me, trying to pull me in another direction, more southwestern. My muscles tensed, preparing for battle, but my spirit yearned.

Patina continued, "The Giants love their farming, their families, and skirmishes. We like our wealth, materialism, and discovery. So when Pops and I clasped hands, it was a moment we were not prepared for."

"And you flew," I concluded. Their flight remained stationary at best.

"No. We floated, as you can see. Somehow, our combined gifts nullified the very forces that keep us firmly on land. We do not know what to call it. We just know we can defy it, and more miraculously, the very force we replaced so we could float, we were able to cast in any direction we wanted." She gave a wry smile. "In this case, we used it to part Quirm's army like the Nesia Ocean as we escaped into the closest cave, thus providing some of our folks with an escape route.

"The divine right is limited in its function, as some of our warriors fell protecting Dwarves and our escape. Now, we were able to make it in, and encounter many Endos who never made it to the execution because of distance."

"I am confused, Patina. I do not understand this thing about Mesos, Endos, and whatnot," I stated.

King Qualt and his "trinket" landed from their floating. His makeshift throne absorbed into his armor as he proceeded to educate me. "There are three different classes in our estate. Three different matrixes. Endo-Dwarves are the miners. They thrive deep in Zaendara's bellows, mining for metals and jewels. Those artifacts are delivered to the Meso-world, where those Dwarves utilize the artifacts in the forges located throughout the region. Those inventions arrive to the Epi-world, where we live. We take and barter them with the Giants and Nixies to maintain a living for the three worlds."

"And Ding? Where does he fit in?"

Uncomfortable, Qualt paused. "Ding. Ding was an Endo. A miner." He paused again.

"What is it, Qualt?"

"We do not know what to do, Eagle. All I can think of doing is protecting our greatest treasures here, especially the cannon. There are more components to the cannon than we showed you."

"What do you think they would do with it?"

"We do not know."

The same psychic tugging pulled on my innards more strongly. I bent my head down, stroking my forehead.

"Are you OK, Eagle?" Patina asked.

"I think. I think my jodepiece is calling me."

Heat . . . heat . . . cold . . . Oh, my piece's menthol coldness tried to overwhelm my body and mind.

"How? How do you know?" Qualt asked.

"I . . . I just do. And where it is, we will find Ding. He may have disowned his spirit in the piece, but my spirit still controls it. We need to go to it."

Qualt scoffed. "With what? We only have enough force to protect what we have here. The rest of these folks are miners. Endos. They would have no idea what to do. Plus, they do not have any—"

"Weapons? King Qualt, you have an incredible arsenal. Your people—y-your folks—I am sure would not have any problem brandishing them if they only had a reason. I say gather them and follow my lead. If Elves can fight for their lives on Quirmean soil, your folks can fight the sparse forces here."

"And the mist?"

I gritted my teeth, trying to hold my anger. "Follow my lead."

Patina beamed with a trace of hope. "The Endo-Dwarves may not be warriors, but they are very hardworking and tenacious. Maybe we Epis could learn something from them." She hesitated. "Tell me, Eagle. What kind of weapon did your Ding brandish?"

"An axe like I have never seen before."

"The blades made of diamonds? The handle of the strongest mahogany?"

"Yes."

"Named Gore?" She smirked.

"Why, yes. So you do know Ding."

"Nolly gee, yes, we do," Patina answered with her best twang.

Patina and Qualt stared at each other as if sharing a secret. Patina proceeded to the exit, her chain-mail tunic jingling loudly with every deliberate step. Qualt scratched a shoulder itch beneath his furred sleeve.

"Come on, Pops, let us help our folks save their heroine."

"Wait," I pleaded, baffled. "Are you talking about Ding? Ding is male."

Patina giggled before opening the door. "No, King Eagle. He is a 'she.'" Patina swung open the door, stepping down the ladder. "Now, share your plan with our folks, and let us go and save her."

* * *

Wyp
Eastern Quirmean city and entertainment center

Aman no longer owned his weaponry shop that was burned down by these rebellious Elves, but at least they pulled him out before he died from the fumes. Being a faithful veteran, Rondo compensated him well for his losses, acknowledging that Aman had saved a painting of Queen Maxis knighting him when he was young.

Ygl & the Dwarf

The former slave owner had decided to retire in Wyp while fretting about that dratted General Ygl stealing his slave Thalla from him. *That Ygl should pay. Thalla was a good slave.*

Unlike in northern Vante, artistic Wyp's war protests moved more like performance art. Despite Aman and many Quirmeans sanctioning deeds influenced by Xurchon, the old veteran heard that certain artists found themselves experiencing revelations. The artists remembered things they had forgotten.

Hence, he decided to attend their roaring achievement, *The Staff and the Shield.* An engrossing play based on Man's deities Istratos and Welna and their mystic weapons, the Staff of Power and the Shield of Creation. According to newspapers, the play's tour felt like a revival, with attendees forced to go on waiting lists for the next performance.

The play returned to Wyp, where even Lorellian slaves were allowed to attend a performance. Their attendance upset Aman, who was too tired to do anything about it.

Everyone witnessed the birth of the Great Wall of Quirm, meant to protect Quirm from the rest of Zaendara. They witnessed Istratos and Welna imbuing Quirm's first royal couple, Emperor Rykon and Empress Hethomes, with their divine right, magic. Aman was sure there were more past members of royalty, but somehow, he couldn't remember.

If General Spenz hadn't been on the battlefield, he'd have made enchanting music. If Prince Antelon hadn't disappeared, he'd have painted the most beautiful scenery and murals. If Princess Jonas hadn't headed a rebellion against her father, she would've been an enchanting lead actress.

If Princess . . . Princess . . . That's weird. Aman couldn't remember the other daughter.

No matter. This night, *The Staff and the Shield* would host another full house at the Grand Theatron, eager to hear a gospel many craved. A world where all races lived as . . . one? In an empire of . . . one?

There was an emperor even more psychotic than Rondo whom no one could remember? *What?*

Intermission came, preparing Aman and the audience for a civil war similar to what was happening now with Princess Jonas.

As the stage curtains closed, some attendees with markings on their foreheads—a hood with a bowl-shaped scoop below and a dot on either side—blocked the exit as some audience members tried to exit the darkening room. *Odd.*

The lighting behind the curtains faded. The only luminance, the twin moons' light slipping through the five-foot windows' curtains on thirty-foot oaken walls.

Galloping horse hooves stampeded from behind the stage curtains. The actors' desperate screams seeped through the cloth, with haunting swords' swishing drenching the air.

Swish-swish. Swish-swish.

"Oh my, Divinity! The show still goes on." An excited attendee beamed.

"Humph," Aman grunted in disbelief.

He glanced at the twenty-foot stage curtains for a surprise, waiting for the lanterns to blaze backstage. Nus and Anul's pale light played on the stage curtains.

No lantern blazed.

The cries lessened sharply; an odd gurgling followed.

Ygl & the Dwarf

A steamy heat blanketed the room.

The shadows on the stage curtains seemed to shift to an unnatural rhythm. What were once images of rooftops and building corners seemed to—merge.

An actress broke through the stage curtain's partition, barely visible. "D-demons. Demons!" She huffed and puffed.

Some attendees applauded her performance.

She's good! She seemed so real, Aman thought.

An errant moonbeam crossed the actress's path on the stage's perimeter, revealing a bloody face and scarred bodice.

Wow! Great makeup.

The shaping shadows on the stage curtains formed into a fifteen-foot centaur with eight legs. Heaving bat wings hoisted the shadowy monster over the actress, who began to run up the aisle.

Aman ran for the door, noticing the horrific reality. A couple of the marked attendees blocked him, holding him tight.

"Don't worry, Xurchon believer," the bigger thug whispered to him. "You are safe. The great god sends his children to teach these nonbelievers a lesson."

"Prophets." The Demon cackled a fiery hiss. "You fashion yourselves prophets?"

"Demons!" the actress screamed before an abundance of blackened blades emerged from the murky beast, slicing her to bits.

"Mersa the Merciless of the Raaligor will show you who the true prophet is." The Demon grinned.

Aman swallowed hard. War had its consequences. He hadn't counted on this being one.

Chapter 20: Uryid

Southern Zaendara, outside the Cory
Mountains
Early morning? Late night?

The days' measure did not matter when the Faerie queens' heavenly bodies fought a celestial battle throughout the starry skies.

The rumbling thunderheads performed their best effort, trying to mask the twin moons' presence.

General Umbala could see Pixy Gasma's largest aquatic toe, a five-foot globe, touching ground and whizzing into a torrential twister of air and water with Juna's divine right.

The waterspout wreaked havoc on the stressed prairie. Muddy chunks exploded everywhere. The novel phenomenon created a small trench, digging deeper into a minor canyon.

Did Inner Earth weep from such pain?

Giantic general Umbala resigned from his battle much like his Ogrean counterpart; the muddy chunks crashed near him as he ran for cover. Evasive tactics were essential at this battle's level. Egos had to be pushed aside. The rain made *tinky-tink-tink* sounds upon his bronze armor.

The transgender general slipped on the ground. A shadow grew around him. He jumped up, ran, and leapt as far as his incredible strength could take him.

Ygl & the Dwarf

A twenty-foot mud ball crashed on a spot near the Giant, coating him.

* * *

Ogrean general Punok's invulnerable skin could withstand much of the earthly assault, but the Ogre knew he did not have the strength to withstand being buried in a sloshing flurry of muddied projectiles.

He dodged and dodged as best he could.

Lightning forks struck faster and faster with greater frequency, causing defiant fires to spring up and spread throughout the dampened field.

The muddied earth was sucked into the vortex, adding to the catastrophe. The thickened twister whipped and struggled on itself and seemed to divert to a more northerly direction, deeper into the Dark Plains.

Lightning bolts danced and wove throughout the twister's upper atmosphere.

If air and water cried in pain, no one heard.

The bolts culminated, shooting down to the ground like snakes slithering through grass, and disseminated throughout the field like a flower with jagged petals—petals refusing to stop.

* * *

Giantic Umbala glanced back to measure his distance from the electrical stream chasing him. He held some distance, but the stream flowed too fast.

He gathered his incredible strength and leapt as high and as far as he could over the twister's conjured canyon.

The electric sea swept beneath him.

* * *

Ogrean Punok stopped, too exhausted from all the running, needing to catch a breath. He saw the sea of power surging toward him, hoping his gift of invulnerability would be enough resistance. At first, he stood proud with broadened chest and wondered how resistant his internal organs would be.

Punok knelt behind his granite shield, gripping his chimaera cloak, realizing the uselessness of this effort against the furious onslaught. *Something needs to give . . .*

He heard a familiar squawk as monstrous talons grasped the link between his granite breastplate and upper armband. Aquiline Pillager repeated a squawk as the faithful gryphon lifted its master to safety.

* * *

In midleap and twist, Umbala noticed the lightning petals halt their surge. The petals receded to and up the tornado at triple the speed, impregnating the swirling summit. The tornado's peak exploded, emitting the most brilliant flash over the Dark Plains and Cory Mountains.

Had Los and Num, the twin suns, broken through?

The amassed armies cowed to the powerful display in the biting wind.

Had the Divinity finally arrived?

A lightning bolt, ten inches thick, emerged from the point of impact. The bolt careened over a small hill, crashing upon the area beyond. A twenty-foot fire flickered in its place; smaller ones danced in the field.

Ygl & the Dwarf

The tornado dissipated in the phenomenon's wake. The winds and rain persisted but stirred at half their strength.

Like weightless leaves, the once-monstrous Faerie queens tumbled in the shifting winds.

Trans-general Umbala's bulky form landed, tripped, and slid into the sloshy mud; the twister's muddy remnants exploded around him. He raised his bronze shield, protecting himself, helpless to do anything for Juna.

The muddy hail ended.

Heat. Had he landed close to one of the bonfires? He peered from behind his shield. Indeed, a fervent bonfire raged—a marvel to behold, considering the moisture everywhere. The bonfire flickered fervently.

Umbala observed it more closely.

Was it taking form?

Where the upper licks flickered, a corona rolled over; a pairing of vacuous eyes appeared.

The Giantic general stumbled rearward, bronzy shield still raised. He shuffled, retreating farther, captivated by the beyond.

Across the fiery creature's backdrop, the other fires evolved into similar smoldering beings.

From behind the small hill, almost central, the hugest fire creature seemed to tower, as if the mixing winds had rolled it up.

The infernal monster sat atop the hill, a fifteen-foot heap, scanning the landscape. A fiery maw emitted a thermal roar.

A hellish creature indeed arrived!

The transgender general knew he needed more than divine strength to overwhelm his new adversary. *Wits. Wits!*

The other creatures roared in response as their leader lurched forward. Two blistering appendages scorched the wet field, helping the leader arise at a stumble.

The Fire Monster blazed another roar. The disciples followed; a fizzing permeated the air as they lumbered from every direction.

Umbala emitted a loud whistle while jogging backward.

* * *

In the air, Fairy Ood, Juna's husband, noticed unconscious Juna and Gasma maintaining a slow drift to the surface—within the Fire Monster's range.

As Ood commanded the air to propel him faster to Juna—his divine right spilling the blackest light from his palms—Pixy First King Guisarrio's four wings dashed to save Gasma.

The curious monster fizzed a little, as if trying to speak, before reaching up to grab the lifeless duo.

Ood and Guisarrio swooped in, clutching their wives from certain danger.

The Fairy king watched as Guisarrio called upon his divine right, shaping the rain into watery spears, casting a volley at the behemoth, distracting it.

In tandem, Ood's piercing black light provided some impairment as the beam tore through the beast's smoldering chest. The beam sucked the chest into an endless void, erupting a ten-foot hole. Unfortunately, a coronal roll sealed the wound.

* * *

"Come to me, beast of the Interim!" General Umbala challenged when he saw the Faerie couples were safe. "Come get me!" He had gathered mud into a ten-foot ball, casting the projectile at the lumbering inferno. Upon contact, a raging explosion ensued.

The creature dissipated into grayish smoke amidst the crumbling rocks.

"Earth." Umbala smirked, more thankful for his gamble than prideful. "Inner Earth's flesh you dare not touch destroys you, monstrosity. It shall become your undoing."

"Wee . . ." gurgled another fifteen-foot attacker fizzing from another direction. A sporadic chorus of infernos repeated this as the assaulter spit a stream of fire from a smoldering maw at Umbala.

Giantic Umbala slashed his sickle-lance into Zaendara, gathering as much mud as possible on the two wide blades. The general jumped back diagonally, dodging the flame. His wielding arm extended as he arched, his thumb searching the staff's ridge for a hidden button, pressing it, releasing the muddied sickles as he swung his arm forward.

The boomerangs soared.

"Wee . . ." the infernal chorale rang.

The new assailant cast another fiery stream at the still-sailing Umbala, but his red pegasus, Slab, rose between the Giant's legs, carrying Umbala to safety with a left swerve.

Caught off guard, the puzzled creature stared at the escapees. The soiled sickles sliced through the creature's posterior, causing much pain.

Hearing the thermal wail, the other animated bonfires wobbled inward.

Slab swooped around. Umbala raised his lance high, the sickles locked into the spiraled grooves atop it; setting in.

"Wee arrrre . . ."

As Slab flew higher to the right, Umbala noticed a familiar Ogrean princess rushing against the blazing assault on her shelled kiradoura.

"Gravelp!" Umbala yelled. He found himself caring for this female, just as exiled as he was.

"I got this, Umbala!" the focused princess responded. "I got this!"

The Fire Monster did not pay her any mind, too fixated on the strident general.

Gravelp leapt off Hogar's Beard's head, calling upon her divine right of destruction. She slammed her heavy fists on the moistened ground. Muddy mounds popped toward their quarry from her divine right's vibrational effect, each mound building bigger and bigger as her vibration expanded from its point of origin.

As if hitting a climatic point, the final mound exploded its earthly assault upon the wobbling monstrosities. Some Fire Monsters diminished into gray wisps. The survivors stared at Gravelp and Umbala in fearful confusion.

"Weeee arrrre . . ." The chorusing echo resounded further.

Another creature shrieked in horror. General Umbala pelted the fiery flesh with stones from a sling, producing more gray wisps with each success.

"Gravelp," the general called from Slab, hovering above her, "help me deflect these monsters from my estate, and I will help deflect them from your Ty Desert."

Gravelp did not answer; their common enemy transfixed her. "What they doing?" she asked in her broken language, trying to fasten her opal-lined headdress.

Ygl & the Dwarf

As if caught in a vortex, the smaller walking bonfires aspirated into the central larger one. With every addition, the central monster grew larger and larger. A towering inferno.

"Weeee arrrre . . ." The inferno tried to speak.

Umbala smirked. "Glory to war, by Lolung-Cor's lance of strength."

"You insane?" Gravelp asked, cowering.

Thrilled, Umbala sliced his sickle-lance deeper through the mud. "Can you not feel the glory of battle, Ogre? If not, then maybe you should go back. Is this not what your barbaric people came here for?"

"No," Gravelp cried, "we thought . . . they thought you attack us."

The Giantic general's eyebrows furrowed with compassion. From behind her, he could see his army rumbling across the puddles and darkened skies to defend the Cory Mountains. A familiar father in tungsten armor on a sable pegasus charged at the vanguard.

"Are you going to help?" Umbala asked her.

"Yes," Gravelp replied, trying to wipe her tears away.

He took his helmet off so that she could witness his rugged features. His cropped hair matched the growing beard he flashed under his visor, his strong jawline set and a confident gentleness in his blue eyes. "Then stay put here while I try to divert this monster into the plains." He winked at her before donning his helmet. "Your Highness." His impassive tone, somewhat endearing.

Umbala guided Slab higher, blowing the war cry on his fancy trumpet, adding a sound the regiments knew very well from training years.

"Weeee arrrre . . . Uryyyyiiiid."

Uryid.

The Fire Monster had a name at last. Though still wobbling, the merged Uryid scanned its surroundings. Was the fifty-foot monster concerned about the tiny Ogre positioned before it?

The Uryid dodged the soiled boomerangs whirring about, but Punok's stones pelted the lower infernal area from the opposite direction.

The Uryid stumbled, chasing the weaving Slab and Pillager to the north.

Pounds of earth partially smothered a foot, striking from the southwest.

* * *

Ogrean King Smush watched the towering inferno stumble as he landed a squawking Dune in the northeast. The dark-skinned lord of the Ty Desert observed piles of earthen debris everywhere, hoping Queen Squash and their people were safe.

Throwing his silken cloak off shoulders burdened with years of service to a thankless populace, Smush raised his hands, beefy pinkies prominent, and curled them as if picking something up—the earthen tonnage collected, rising to the air.

Smush's forces halted their descent behind him. They knew their king's divine right and awaited the verdict as the slick loads meshed into two halves of a makeshift tomb.

* * *

From the canyon's south side, Giantic King Erosc grimaced, witnessing his Ogrean counterpart's feats. He raised his arm, bent at the elbow, forearm turned down. The vanguard forces saw Erosc's signal and trumpeted his order to desist.

Ygl & the Dwarf

The determined king landed Shadocoat and searched deep within himself for the very energies his divine right bestowed on him. He raised his hands, index fingers prominent. Bones broke and reformed. Cartilage popped and reshaped. Skin and muscle stretched and reconstructed, his paraphernalia enlarging collectively. Once his height was attained, it almost matched the Uryid's.

"Weeee arrrre—"

"I know what you are, creature," Erosc boomed, snarling. The blaze's reflection morphed on his tungsten panoply. "Now, go back to the Interim's pits that spawned you."

He bent to the makeshift gulley, scooping as much muck as he could.

* * *

The shocked Uryid gasped, a flaming puff popping out. Being surrounded from three directions, its fate became clear.

The Uryid turned to flee into the Dark Plains.

The Death Mist floated before the frightened monster, blocking it. At first apprehensive, the Uryid assessed the new spangled adversary with an alarmed curiosity. Stumbling back in fear, the fiery monster found itself further studying the pale mist fluctuating above the tall grasses. Mist and fire impervious to the storm.

The mist waited.

The Uryid quivered, sensing something powerful and unsettling. Something the monster was not yet prepared to face. With fear and fury, an angry fizz erupted from the beast. Unbearable heat emanated from it, drying the land within a ten-foot radius. Upon the radius, a small fire formed, erupting into a coronal wall of flames protecting its master.

* * *

Erosc pitched his massive mud ball.

Smush allowed his tomblike walls to collide, but before Smush's enclosure could seal the sizzling barrier, a monstrous fireball rocketed from within the flaming fence, shooting into the heavens, veering toward the southeast stratus: the Uryid was escaping.

Smush and Advisor Crumb cast as much divined earth as possible to obstruct the fireball's trajectory. The Ogres on flying gryphons assisted in slinging stones while their brethren below raised granite shields to block shrapnel.

From his best vantage point, Erosc observed the fireball's arc. "It is going south to the Urvan Sea," the forty-foot royal boomed for all to hear.

The comet seared into the thunderheads, as if preparing to scorch the heavens—never to be heard from again.

Chapter 21: The Dwarven Thief

Zak, the Dwarven capital
The Grand Core

Ding struggled hard against internal pain on the damp turf.

Quirmean general Spenz and a small gathering of troops surrounded her outside the Core. The Dwarven thief had no idea how often she fell into unconsciousness or how she was able to withstand the jodepiece she held for so long.

"Xur-Xurchon . . . help m-me," the atheist pleaded to the nonresponding deity.

She had upheld her end of the bargain, retrieving the Elvin general for him. It was not her fault Xurchon had failed so miserably in capturing the Elf.

This power, she thought to herself. *How did the Elf ever overcome it?*

In the early-morning light, she lay trembling upon the grasses like a baby, struggling against the piece's power, before a thirty-foot mouth of a cave. The piece's menthol coolness swathed her with ill intent.

A gilded archway adorned the cave's mouth, blended with brass and platinum contours, seeming to relay a story no one understood from its etchings. Ding could finally understand some of the archway's motifs through her delirium. From the archway's lower left side, the creatures with pointy ears and their rotund allies with clubs were Elves and Ogres fighting Quirmeans and monsters in a forest.

The Forest of Lorel?

Traveling up the arch, miserable Ding perceived the Dwarven army fleeing this battle, but as her line of sight approached the arch's summit, she witnessed the army combining with the Giants in the mountains. At the arch's summit, both armies fought the monsters.

Moving down from the summit, Ding deciphered Demons' misshapen forms. A huge Demon led the grotesque mob, moving against the etchings' direction, against waiting images of what could only be deciphered as regal Giants and Dwarves.

The next image portrayed a fiercer battle with this new enemy. In the next image, a regal Giant smashed the huge Demon to its demise with a huge club—but Giants did not use clubs.

Near the archway's end, Ding deciphered Demons and monsters fleeing the energized forces, retreating back into the fabled Unknown Land. The relief terminated on the right with winning armies guarding the mountains' borders.

This could not be true. Only the Giants guarded the Cory's borders. The Dwarven thief struggled with too much pain to fully understand this monument.

Her shivering pupils witnessed Spenz and his troops nearing. They snickered in their Quirmean steel. And from beyond her vantage point, even more groupings of soldiers.

Where the Epi-Dwarves hid, she did not know. The few she eyed toiled as slaves, stripped of all the fancy armor and paraphernalia the Meso-

Ygl & the Dwarf

Dwarves had forged for them with material found by her class, the Endos.

She did not care, though. Aside from trying to get rid of this dratted jodepiece, all the ruddy thief cared about at this moment was one thing.

"Wh-where i-is he?" she demanded.

"That's a good question, Dwarf. Where exactly is he? The Elvin general?" Spenz asked, fiddling with his flute.

"I do not know. You had your chance to use him for whatever . . ."

"You're correct, but that was when we were searching for the jodepiece."

"I have it," Ding squealed, tears flowing. "I have it!"

"Where?" The Quirmean general peered closer.

"Take it! Take it!" Her trembling right fingers unfurled on the grass to reveal . . .

"Nothing." Spenz grimaced in his visor, squatting. "You show me nothing, thief. Are you losing sight of your skills?"

"N-n-no. Take it. Please."

Spenz pulled on Ding's quivering limbs. "Nothing. I see nothing, Dwarf. What kind of fool do you take me to be?"

Ding whimpered, pulling her furled hand closer to herself. "It. Is. Here."

Spenz calmly stood, observing his troops behind him surveying the ordeal, wondering why his eldest brother, Emperor Rondo, didn't just let him do away with this squatty race with a quick whistle on his flute.

Taking off his steel helmet in the clearing sky, he gazed north at Pariot's Trumpet, an eighty-foot volcano looming in the distance. With outstretched arms, the sarcastic general addressed the surrounding troops. "Well, has anybody seen it? A little sparkling jewel? A strange little trinket?"

Silence.

"No?" He encircled trembling Ding, examining her before kicking her stomach. "Where is it? Where is it?" Spenz yelled. "Why are you here? Why are you here?"

"Stop. Stop!" Ding cried.

"Why?"

"Stop!"

A brilliant flash of bluish-yellow energy exploded between them, tossing General Spenz into a gaggle of soldiers. Rondo's bewildered brother jumped back to his feet, excited. "What was that?"

"Th-the Jode . . . the jodepiece. Take it."

Spenz rushed to the unfurled hand, exposing the piece's bluish-yellow energy sputtering around it.

"Wh-where is my Dong?" Ding demanded. "Where is my Dong?"

The excited Quirmean slammed into an invisible wall before reaching the Dwarven thief, plopping him on the ground again.

Behind Spenz, his baffled guards regarded weaponry's clattering emitting from deep within the Grand Core's mouth accompanied with explosions and desperate cries.

Chapter 22: Ygl's Charge

My spirit's returning fullness tickled me with a touch of Ding's, smelling like hateful sweat with a bit of grime, as I strategized with Patina and her father on our ascent.

My tainted spirit pulled and tugged at me again, almost as if not letting go of Ding.

Wait. Familiar temperature changes began fluctuating in me. Heat and cold . . . heat and cold.

No doubt. My jodepiece called to me through Ding as well. That part of my humanity hidden within my piece acknowledged the danger it faced and took steps to protect itself.

Poor Ding. Yes, I was disappointed in Ding. And angry, but anger was not getting us anywhere at this point. My Soft Winds meditation was of the utmost importance.

Once calm, I felt so sorry for the awful mistake he—I meant "she"—had made in stealing my piece. I meant "the" piece.

I knew the difficulty in maintaining control of such power; I still called it "mine" when the piece clearly wanted control. I only hoped my humanity would be enough to protect him—I meant "her."

Oh, this newfound information about her sex played havoc with me. In the Forest of Lorel, we did not have an issue with this distinction. I mean, yes, pretty males and handsome females thrived there; however, our females never had a problem with hairiness. Ding's sex was not an intolerance issue. Understanding reigned here.

But, by Achal, that beard! I could not grow one even if I prayed for it.

My essence called to me, and I believed we might have a chance at more than retrieving the piece. We could possibly save the Dwarven estate or, at least, begin a revolution, especially if we saved Ding, a muse to her people.

And an atheist. A person who did not believe in the existence of any Divinity. Yet, he—she—had witnessed Ethnel, the Essence of Preservation; evoked her Divinities' names; and—I shudder even to think—evoked Xurchon's name.

How did she change? Why?

In the Forest of Lorel, we had atheists, though only a few. Of course, anyone who had never seen their gods and goddesses could abandon faith, but these days, faith was all anyone had left. Yet I admired how much faith her people had in her. A lowly thief—a lowly, angry thief.

The moment Patina let them know Ding had not met death, the Mesos and Endos became enthused. Bygones became bygones, even with Patina telling them to listen to my orders. These pale or ruddy Dwarves—some more so than others—untidy in appearance and stinky like Ogres—well, some more so than others . . .

The ruddier Dwarves piled into the spectral cannon's hull with new spirit, plopping readily on the benches and, on command, began turning what Patina called "axle rods" sticking out from the sides. These rods attached to "gears," which, in turn, rotated the wooden wheels.

We moved out of the platinum-walled Northern Forge and into a more familiar earthy terrain. I could only imagine the terrain was a decoy to discourage unwanted visitors.

Ygl & the Dwarf

Zak, their capital, our destination.

These Meso-Dwarves, these smiths, known for their immense strength despite their stockiness, did not let up on the energy needed to get us there. When the first group tired out, another replaced them while Patina steered at the wheel.

In the spectral cannon's surroundings, Wolf and Tole Riders guarded against Quirmean surprises.

The pace was urgent on these smoothed roads, leading us through back channels lined with iron tiles and bright oil lamps.

Some routes were not taken—smaller routes with carts on tracks. The carts were attached to what Patina called "cables." The cables led the Endo-Dwarves in these carts to mines deep in the earth, where they acquired the valuable resources the Meso-Dwarves forged into inventions.

The surface-dwelling Epi-Dwarves used these inventions for trade with the Giants and Nixies. Some of these inventions the Epi-Dwarves used themselves, like the armor they wore and the weaponry.

Since Epi-Dwarves consisted of the royal family, they felt superior to the other two classes, keeping them out of view, using the royal family's divine right as a way to keep the Mesos and Endos in line, treating them like lower-class citizens.

I could understand why the lower classes hated the Epis so much. The Epis enjoyed the fruits of their labor while they endured horrible working conditions. The smiths and miners barely saw the outer world. Inequity, not a pretty word. Ding, my betrayer, the only glue that kept these classes together.

At my direction, some Tole Riders sped farther ahead in the cave; the toles' sonar *wa-wa* could catch the enemy's presence quicker than my infravision. A sonar, according to Patina, was an echo that would bounce back to the half-blind toles once it hit a target. The echo's strength would inform the tole of the object's hardness. Anything soft and fleshy would give off a light sonic. So far, the sonics felt hard.

I hated to admit our pace slowed, but it did. We had covered much distance, but even the sturdy Dwarves tired. Every so often, the groups outside and inside exchanged places.

Qualt mused, "The cannon is not perfect."

I sensed my piece becoming stronger the closer we got to our destination. I suggested, "Then maybe, King Qualt, Patina and you should add your divine right in hurrying the pace."

Qualt grunted.

"Well, nolly gee," Patina responded happily with a wink. "I forgot you are a general too. Welcome to our ranks."

Qualt did not seem to complain.

With a clasping of hands, the newfound power lightened the cannon's weight, relieving the Dwarven rowers. The duo stayed careful not to expend too much energy, knowing their divine right would be needed later.

Soon we drove into familiar earthy terrain. No more tiles. The only lanterns to combat the darkness were held by perimeter insurgents while Tole Riders guarded the upper arena. Plant roots dangled from above, probably the type Patina liked to chew.

"I am amazed Man has not attacked on giant bats and spiders," Qualt mused.

"I believe bats are not about to give away their positions with their screeches, and Spider

Riders are probably positioned near the entrances," I advised.

Patina continued. "At the invasion's beginning, Man attacked the caves' interiors, wielding torches for light, but they realized their venture to be fruitless when they encountered our entrenched forces."

"The Quirmeans will wait for us to emerge for sustenance around the cave's entrance," Qualt added.

"We will be prepared," I concluded.

Our enemy did as we expected, the bats being the primary force—flapping fury hitting with passion.

I hoped my clairvoyance would come into effect. I guessed my new divine right did not work in this manner. *Must I wait for worse matters for my gift to take effect?* Advisor Sylvia was the expert with this divine right. She would have been a great teacher.

Nevertheless, my allies and I could see the approaching light and hear the sudden scurrying.

"What is that?" I asked, my sharp hearing catching something. "Coming from behind. Getting louder."

Like a hundred roaches on the cave's walls and ceiling, the scurrying grew louder behind the cannon.

I peered out the back window. Warped ochre eyes. Hundreds of them flickered. Long wild hair flailed from snickering heads.

"Ditchightls," Patina warned. The limber creatures were like jackrabbits bouncing around each other.

I shivered, remembering my encounter with this awkward adversary.

Patina continued, worried, "Nolly gee, their touch will send us to Xurchon's womb."

"I encountered one at the Ogrean kingdom."

"All the way over there? How did you defeat it?"

"Welbern devoured it."

Patina gasped. "Demonslayer?"

"These soulless monsters share a bond among themselves." Her eager father joined the conversation. "They must have sensed their brother's demise and feared your mystic sword. But they have someone else they disdain as well."

"Pops, do not!" Patina sensed the cannon's weight returning because of their unclasped hands.

"We are almost there, my little jewel." The sixty-year-old crawled up the ladder to the cannon's hatch and opened it, his upper body sticking out. "The Meso- and Endo-Dwarves can take us the rest of the way with Eagle's guidance. I am sure Man has an idea what is occurring now. Let me give the dreaded ditchightl something else to fear."

Indeed he did. Exploding daylight seared around the cannon and his forces. Darkness's denizens shrieked in anger from the brightness pushing them back with Qualt's divined spears.

Qualt laughed. "The nasty beasts hate light. Where there is light, their healing powers fail."

"For sure, they will be waiting for us inside," Patina added.

"Let them." Qualt guffawed, returning his attention to the ditchightls, casting more glowing spears, laughing more. "You thought I was dead!" he yelled at them in his wheezing way. "You monkey roaches!"

We sped on.

Ygl & the Dwarf

Nothing could ambush us because I directed the Tole Riders, in staggered formation, to sense assaults. Plus, Dwarven encampments awaited at the perimeter, upset about Man's incursion. Maybe already there. Maybe the encampments heard the toles' *wa-wa* and came to investigate the scouts' teasing swoops pulling Quirm's hidden Bat Riders from secret havens. Whatever the reason, luck aligned with our side, making me wonder if Gnomic chief Mitral was flying lucky Jinx nearby.

"You are right, King Eagle," Qualt mused. "Man's Spider and Bat Riders are already at the ready. Quirm's forces will not be waiting outside."

We sped on.

These Meso-Dwarves, incredible with their workmanship. They and their Endo compatriots would do anything to save their Ding, including following Patina's and my orders. They allowed the more experienced Epi warriors to lead their ranks as everyone was provided an extraordinary weapon created from "Pariot's Knowledge."

For instance, flaming axes repelled the giant bats' formidable dives. Many Epi Wolf Riders at the vanguard wore bilateral harnesses entailing two sets of small axes—tomahawks—strapped front to back. With both hands, the warriors slapped their tomahawks against a strip on their flanks, sparking a wild flame. What an incredible invention!

With a shout, the frontline Epi-Dwarves threw their flaming tomahawks at Man's Bat Riders. The Wolf Riders swerved in lateral opposing directions, like a peeling banana, providing room for the Tole Riders who followed to attempt to hit more marks.

"The forge-smith Mesos taught the Epis how to use their weapons," Patina informed me, "but the

179

Epis never trained the Mesos in ambidexterity. The Mesos can only hold their weapons in one hand. We regret not teaching them."

But the warriors did not stop there. Even as the Tole Riders fanned out wider and wider, they made sure to keep slinging flaming tomahawks in the outskirts if they thought they caught a Bat Rider fluttering or Man's Spider Riders scaling walls.

Maybe even a ditchightl. Roach monkeys. Ha! What a name Qualt had given them.

Dwarves moving in the inner ranks held their ground, attacking enemies who escaped the primary offense.

The Wolf Riders lashed out against the Spider Riders using the same formation.

The Quirmeans had no idea what had hit them. Our defense quickly became our offense. Even if a tomahawk missed its quarry, my telepathy commanded the second-wave Dwarves to cast their weapons far enough inward and upward for the ensuing fallout to strike the opposition from above.

My jodepiece's evil entity tried washing over me the closer we came, trying to control me, the feeling more overwhelming than before. The coolness . . . its menthol coolness . . .

So inviting . . .

And yet, the defiant heat became what I needed. My essence, mixed with Swen's protection spell, resided in the piece, shielding me from its entity.

You could not control me before, my piece. You will not now.

This moment, most urgent.

Through my connection to the crystalline jodepiece, an image appeared. A man? Short, dark hair and a beard and armor, resembling Emperor Rondo, but not. A flute dangled from his belt.

Spenz? General Spenz! In multifaceted images but Spenz, nonetheless.

My jodepiece's magical coolness tried washing over me more and more as I approached. I shivered, almost keeling over; a strange static electricity rattled me. Why would my piece try to hurt me again with my protective humanity hidden within it? Maybe fear? Fear of General Spenz?

My Achal, my essence feared Spenz! My jodepiece needed me as much as the Jode needed it!

I searched deep within me, searching for Prince Rolando's gift: telekinesis. The Dwarven rowers needed the assist anyway with the loss of their royalties' combined power.

My dead nephew's divine right flowed easily from me—not too much, though. My telekinesis nudged the cannon faster with more vigor than Umbala's divine strength.

"King Qualt, take your seat," I urged during the sudden jolt.

My jodepiece lapped over me in stronger, exhilarating waves as Qualt did so. Patina ran to the controls.

Fascinating. The only Quirmeans attacking were cavalry. No foot soldiers could be detected by my heightened Elvin sense and Qualt's light-blue luminance. Quirm had not expected such an offense from us. Maybe the Quirmeans relied too heavily on the legends, believing Dwarves to be more materialists than warriors. However, today, Dwarves had a strong cause to fight for and a chance to break belief. They might not have been Giants, but these Mesos, Endos, and Epis demonstrated a lot of heart, despite Man's prowess.

The twin suns' looming light became ever more welcoming. These caves' darkness was pretty tiring.

Our last phalanx parted, allowing us through with a hearty contingency covering our flanks and rear.

Despite our thrust, my jodepiece's call hammered me in bigger waves.

"I have to go ahead of you," I warned Patina and Qualt. "My piece's call is becoming too strong. I must go now!"

"Go," stern Qualt ordered. "May your and our Divinity be with you."

Slowly, I diminished my telekinetic push against the cannon's rear. As my divine right's strength subsided, the mighty rowing Mesos and Endos chanted Ding's name. At first, their chant flowed with a low breath, followed by several more. Each statement grew louder and bolder than before, building into a momentous unison.

"Ding. Ding. Ding! Ding!"

The influence this thief had over her people amazed me.

Through the cannon's swinging door, I shot out over the onslaught, bathing in telekinetic energy. Like a feather, my newfound divine right jolted me forward effortlessly to the cave's opening. An expanding spider's webbing blocked my exit.

"Ding. Ding. Ding! Ding!"

Flaming tomahawks flitted in the air on either side of me, wheeling campfires bursting against their intended targets.

A ten-foot spider hurtled from my left past our offense, baring fangs dripping noxious poison. My psionics reached into the monster's bristling hide and, with my outstretched hands' opening, ripped through the spider's sinewy fibers, tearing the eight-legged body asunder. Before most of the bristling shards could escape me, I collected them in a telekinetic sphere, thrusting them through an advancing bat and master.

"Ding. Ding. Ding! Ding!"

How simple! But could my dead brother's divine rights be getting stronger, or was my jodepiece enhancing Methelo's gift?

How satisfying.

I envisioned various images of General Spenz kicking and hitting poor Ding through my jodepiece's facets, as if I was sitting within the crystalline walls, watching.

How dare you, Spenz!

In my mind, I could see myself thrusting Spenz away from my thieving friend through these facets.

My breathing became heavier but not labored. Heavier. Deeper.

Bluish-yellow energy sweated and sparkled out of my pores. I could see nothing but hues of blue and yellow everywhere, as if I had become the Jode.

I blasted past webby canopies shot at me, telekinetically thrusting them back to their origins.

Below, the Wolf Riders retrieved jeweled shields from their back harnesses. Elliptical on top, the shields' concave bottoms fit the tenacious wolves' shoulder harnesses. The Endos and Mesos ran out of tomahawks, unlike the strategic Epis, whose frontline forces pulled out bulky double-headed axes.

Images of Spenz rushed back at Ding. I cast an immediate telekinetic shield up to block the baffled general. It felt so good feeling Spenz smashing against my barrier.

I spun through the air, through the dense webbing created to trap the Dwarves in a supposed massacre. My telekinetic energy attached the webbing to me, my psionic energy seething through the gossamer strands.

Quirm did not think another general would help lead this charge. They did not think the Dwarves' true leader was the female they kicked and beat.

I soared out of the cave and into daylight, dragging a large gaggle of Quirmean soldiers with the seized webbing into a perplexed bunch of others.

Oh, the joy of my accomplishments, floating above them, smothered in pride, arms outstretched, gloating down at them with their emperor's demeanor, the static electricity chilling my veins.

My childhood playmate, General Spenz, had not really acknowledged me yet, too intent on using his divine right over music, blowing into his flute, playing a striking tune. Exhausted Ding lay below him. A certain mystical energy popped off him, intent on destroying my barrier protecting my Dwarven friend, for this was Man's divine right.

Not telekinesis. Not ani-speak. Not white light. Not hypergrowth.

Magic. The ability to tap into the metaphysical and manipulate it in any way desired. Emperor Rondo was the most powerful and feared anyone had known. This was why the Forests of Lorel and Khun had formed a fragile alliance for a strategy we had little belief in, especially Lorel, leaving us too relaxed in our northern defense—too relaxed.

Then again, without my jodepiece, who could withstand Man's Death Mist?

Nonetheless, regret had to be replaced with the matter at hand.

Spenz finally saw me. He played his mystic tune with more intent, his divine right flaring about him like loose musical notes.

"Running into invisible walls brings back memories, does it not, General Spenz?" I asked.

Quirmean squads raced from everywhere toward me. In the distance, I glimpsed a population of Dwarves imprisoned within a large fence.

The Quirmean Bat Riders zoomed in fast.

"Just the person I was looking for," melodic Spenz answered. He witnessed the bluish-yellow sweat oozing out from my pores. "That jodepiece isn't meant for you."

"Well, you are welcome to take it if you like." My voice changed—deeper, darker. "Ding, drop it."

With convulsive shakes, my Dwarven friend's palm allowed my piece to slide off onto the grass.

Bat Riders zoomed around me with notched arrows. Purple lasers zipped past me.

Wait. This was a vision!

I lowered myself, enclosing myself in an array of bluish-yellow sparkles. The Bat Riders' arrows dissolved before they could reach me. Above me, the cannon's lasers shot at advancing Bat Riders, encasing them in individual icy shells, prisons that fell to the ground, injuring or killing hapless soldiers in an explosion of frosty shrapnel.

I still floated in a T formation, turning to observe Spider Riders scampering out of the colony of cave mouths and into grassy knolls, with more Bat Riders following.

Excited Wolf Riders exploded from the Grand Core in a hail of flaming tomahawks and raised shields. Tole Riders ended the exiting parade, flocking up the mountainside after the Spider Riders or steering toward the Bat Riders. The sheer numbers of smelly, sweaty Mesos and Endos bowled over the Quirmean soldiers at the scene. Epi-Dwarves, the most proficient warriors, rolled over the Quirmeans they perceived to be the most threatening, alleviating the less experienced Dwarves of any mishaps.

The mighty Quirmeans had no idea what had hit them. Spenz had allotted so much effort to directing his forces into every available entry, he had not suspected Dwarven gutsiness or actual numbers in one area.

Could his God of Evil not have warned them?

The earth started to shudder, knocking some off-balance. The laser cannon muscled through the cavern's adorned mouth. Patina positioned herself on top; eight Dwarves surrounded her, bearing shields.

Though at a distance, my Lorellian vision could perceive her voluptuous form's slight shiver, the fear on her face. Her outstretched arms clasped before her, a ball of molten magma swishing on the other end.

The poor princess was not made for war—so used to much finer things . . .

An anger swelled within me unlike any I had ever felt before.

"Princess! Patina! You stupid ditchightl's wart!" My seething sending pierced through her, startling her. *"They took your kingdom from you. Take it back! Give them no mercy as they gave you none."*

Patina shivered more. *"I . . . I cannot kill others."*

"Who do you think rode those stupid spiders and bats? Kill them. Chimaera's dung!"

Ygl & the Dwarf

With a scream and a sob, the frightened princess focused her magma blast on incoming Bat Riders.

Oh, the ecstasy, sensing her complete fear. The molten earth's fallout even burned a few Dwarves—exhilarating!

Oh, the joy. The incredible joy to kill and kill and kill. I enjoyed the killing while draped in my bluish-yellow haze.

No matter how many Quirmeans raced to quell the sudden uprising, it was too late. The Dwarven offensive proved too strong and too many. The Quirmeans were mauled over.

And I enjoyed every moment of their barrage from my vantage point.

The terrain stopped shaking.

A flute?

Yes, a flute's symphony. A most melodious sound, though harsh in tone. A mystic barrier, like a plane of rising rain, arose from the ground, separating Man from Dwarf, cutting through whoever trudged across its way.

Unlucky captors from both races found themselves trapped on either side.

My floating body rotated to investigate the melodic source: wonderful Spenz. He played a slightly different note, transforming his abandoned soldiers into rising rain, teleporting them back to his side of his barrier. The Dwarven warriors on his side did not meet the same fate as they fought valiantly on their war wolves.

I did not raise a hand to help those Dwarves. Instead, I remained floating in their direction, soaking in the scent of enthralling deaths. The invigorating smell mixed well with my intoxicating piece's magic—all this power merging with my divine right.

Oh. Oh, the joy . . .

A reedy *wa-wa*.

No need to rotate for that.

"What are you doing?" Patina, startled, hovered behind me on silvery-black Twilight from the barrier's other side, with escorts joining her. "Nolly gee, save them. Bring them back to me," she yelled.

"Silence!" My psionic admonishment seethed into every mind in my nearby radius.

I relished their pain. Relished their tears.

Reeling, Patina pleaded, "Stop it. Stop it."

Most of the Dwarven warriors trapped on my new side—Spenz's side—were Epi.

Apparently, some Dwarves on Patina's side did not notice Spenz's barrier because they continued with their charge until others alerted them. The Epi warriors tried to command their lesser comrades to fall back into formation, but after so many years of classism, those commands fell on ignorant ears. Instead, the Mesos and Endos who found Ding yelled her name and continued riding to her defense, to their end.

The cautious Quirmeans had already noticed their musical general's barrier.

My jodepiece, Spenz, and Ding stirred below me. "Back off," I promptly commanded. "This artifact is mine."

How easy. My bluish-yellow sweat popped off me, with an expeditious frothing through the air, fencing in the Dwarven warriors on my side and a few Quirmeans within a spangled barrier.

How exhilarating to feel myself surrounding me, my essence reaching into those sweat particles, forcing them to grow and change into a semblance of me. Not an exact semblance—more of a transparent silhouette—but definitely me.

Brave Spenz stared at me—sword at hand, flute in mouth.

"Please, Ygl," Ding pleaded softly, her vulnerable body a quivering mass, lying there near him. Defeated. No diamond-headed Gore. No wolf Redfang.

Just her.

"Save them," she tried sending.

Her plea struck me. Never had I heard or felt her in this manner. The fool. How could she ever believe she could control my jodepiece?

The doomed Dwarven contingent gathered into a small formation, creeping backward toward my spangling field's leeward side, feeling a sense of protection.

The hesitant Quirmean army outside my barrier swelled much less, noticing my bluish-yellow spangles. With a slight gesture, I extended my essence to the abandoned Dwarves, protecting them further.

I did not understand why I did that; I did not really care for them.

They were not what I came for.

I turned my attention to my childhood friend Spenz, positioned at the ready.

"The jewel is mine, Ygl," Man's general commanded. "It goes with me, as well as you, back to Quirm."

Am I just surrounded by fools?

"Go ahead, Spenz." I glided down, facing him. "From a king to a general, I give the jodepiece to you."

He examined me, sizing me up, blowing a soft whistle.

The air up and down and around me crackled and sloshed. I found myself within a writhing, mystic binding.

I smiled warmly at my old friend. "Go," I whispered.

With brash confidence, Spenz swiped my fragment lying three feet away from the Dwarven thief, examining the tiny artifact.

He looked at me as he touched and felt it.

I could feel him touching and feeling me.

"Spenz, remember when we played hide-and-seek all those years ago?" I queried.

He sneered. "That was a different Spenz. A stupid boy who wanted your friendship."

"You cheated, remember?"

"Wanting you to find me wasn't cheating, idiot."

"But the game was to hide until I found you. See? I returned the favor. I let you find me."

Spenz looked at me, confused. He should have sensed my trap. I believed his ego was too big.

He continued. "By right of the Quirmean Empire and emperor—argh!"

More of my essence trickled from my piece into his vulnerable palm, sailing through his arm's every vessel, tickling my favorite area, his mind. There, I searched his mental pathways' nooks and crannies, soaking up every morsel I could find, taking over his mind.

"Peek-a-boo."

As a telepath, I already knew these arenas. It was not hard for me.

Ygl & the Dwarf

I traveled toward his memories, connective memories that helped me see through his eyes, his world becoming a bluish-yellow twinkle.

I could visualize myself through Spenz—united by his divine right—our mystic transference phenomenal, his body's webbing engrossing, like a new outfit.

Through him, I witnessed my physical being, my "Me," stepping through his dissolved binding, Me lifting his vulnerable form slightly off the ground with telekinesis, sensing his fear and tension.

I was in and yet before him, two places at once. I bathed in his discomfort while watching it.

I dove into his lungs.

"Go ahead, Spenz," Me encouraged him, approaching him through the bluish-yellow haze exploding from both our eyes. "Try to whistle out of this," Me challenged.

General Spenz fell to his knees, choking, as I soared into his mind's lateral portion to chew on new memorial morsels.

And there Spenz strode, in a morsel, whistling a frosty breath, walking through an elder Dwarf's faint violet light, raising his Quirmean steel against Advisor Eifner's shield of fragile ice.

In another morsel, Dwarven general Ilinor, a much younger version of Qualt, defied Spenz firmly in the memorial haze within a metallic shelling much like his Dwarven father's, wielding an axe similar to Ding's Gore.

Another memory presented Spenz/Me riding hurriedly with his/my army through a teleporting vortex.

Another memory: Spenz/Me holding the Lamp of Swen in his/my palm, staring at it in thought, slapping it into his/my saddle's side, dangling from a rope in a forest.

Another memory: two males and a female argue with him/me. Two brothers and a sister, maybe? Somehow, I'm drawn to the brother with shorter hair. But Spenz is Rondo and Werkle's younger brother. Nephews and niece? Rondo's children! The empty thrones in Rondo's throne room.

Another memory: Spenz/I close a dungeon door on a whimpering silhouetted figure sprawled on the ground.

Another memory: I/Spenz witness Xurchon casting hoary energy at one of the brothers, who defends himself with a raised card before being disintegrated. The sister, astonished, looks on.

Another memory: I/Spenz stands behind Rondo on a balcony in Gablen as Rondo pontificates to a massive audience.

Another memory: I/Spenz bows to Xurchon in a room brimming with billowy white smoke.

"No! You will not have me!" I shook in utter shock and with heavier gasps. The thought of worshipping such evil contempt sickened me.

My corporeal being scrutinized vulnerable Spenz who was paralyzed within the bluish-yellow gaze I created while thriving in him. Spenz, so very close to Me, my corporeal being.

"Give that to me," Me stated, my outstretched hand as stern as my voice.

His clenched fist opened with a snap; my jodepiece ripped off his palm, leaving a bloody smear.

No telekinesis. No magic. My piece traveled of its own accord. My piece was meant to be with— Me.

Ygl & the Dwarf

When my piece landed on my right palm, it sunk into Me, the effect reminding Me of the weed schlepper sucking into me during the Dark Plains ambush. A peppy onrush struck Me like never before.

Cold . . .

So. Much. Menthol cold.

Too much cold . . . but where's the heat?

My essence stole away from unconscious Spenz, returning to fulfill my incomplete spirit floating within my jodepiece's brilliant matrix—

Something was wrong. My essence no longer belonged to me. My essence had somehow become tainted by my sneaky piece.

My piece was controlling my actions all the while!

My floating half spirit must have absorbed my piece's foul influence in the matrix. My half spirit, meant to buffer the Party and me from Xurchon!

My eyes squinted in the effort to contain the assailing energy, hoping the other Party members remained safe.

Oh, my Achal, I needed the heat.

My hijacked spirit kept eating into me, trying to change me.

My jodepiece finally outwitted me, using my anger toward Spenz to control me, and I fell for the deceit. I became so focused on Spenz, I left myself vulnerable to the piece's sentience.

Crippled, I found myself struggling.

The heat finally arrived, but not the type I expected.

Welbern wailed in defiance, hovering above, my sword's amber flames licking through my trendy clothes, trying to burn through them to my sneaky invader, but my piece kept repairing the damage.

"I am here, Ygl. Do not fear." That voice. That syrupy voice. Sweet and intoxicating like morning dew off a brown sugar lily. *"Thou is not alone in a place so drear."*

"S-Swen. I did not call you."

"Thou did. I could feel thee in the grid."

My squinting eyes peeked from my hunched posture on the ground. Her twinkling obsidian gases swirled about me, tickling Welbern and my skin, obscuring the piece's bluish-yellow spangle. Her dismembered presence—still not enough—sidled away from Demonslayer.

"F-fight it, Ygl," Ding raged. "Only you can."

"Help me, Swen. I need help," I begged.

"Master Ygl, relax," my enigmatic genie soothed. *"Let the moment pass."*

"I-I . . . am so c-cold."

"I know. I know. It is the Jode," she soothed further. Her sympathetic gases curled closer around me, unfurling me from my protective hunch. Her brazen fingertips felt my cheek, turning my head toward her hollow eyes, reminding me of our cherished moment in the Forest of Khun. *"As I feel, I begin to heal. I am here to dissipate thy fear. The strength thou must find is in thy mind."*

The heat . . .

The incredible heat seared into me. Swen was correct. I had to fight this doppelganger, this deceit, in my fractured soul intertwining with my psyche.

Swen could not perform this act alone. I almost regretted leaving half my humanity within my piece, but I needed to in order to survive Xurchon and Rondo's assault in the Dark Plains, in order to protect the Party of the Jode.

Amber flames burst like new clothes on me, crackling but not searing my feeble flesh. Welbern, my Demonslayer, hovered above me, wrapped in Swen's obsidian gases and chiming runes, casting flame upon amber flame, trying to quench the jodepiece's evil out of me.

And their help seemed to work. The combined enchantments sliced into my invader's possession from various angles, providing me a glimpse of hope.

Again, I reached deep through the slices, into my being's core, to search for my last ounce of strength, for some spark of life.

I found her—my beloved wife, Thalla—smiling down on me, touching me, kissing me, and caressing me. Limbus hugged my leg. Estranged Steadfast nuzzled me. We were all so happy, playing in a small Lorellian field.

So happy.

I chased Limbus down the daisy field and tackled him on healthy grass, laughing playfully.

Thalla arrived next to us, with equine Steadfast lying in the background.

I jumped up to kiss my beloved wife.

And found myself kissing Swen.

Sweet, intoxicating Swen.

We were so happy together.

Hope.

Steadfast snorted a roaring neigh that seemed so real.

"You cannot. You will not control me. I am my own person!" I challenged my piece.

As the unbearable heat tore a few more slices into my piece's menthol cold, I found my true self shattering through the cracks. "I control you. I. Am. Your. Master."

Freedom. True freedom. That powerful word called to me.

The deceit began to fail. I ripped through the cracks. The true me. The real me. The deceit tried to retain me, tried to hold me, but I would not allow it.

"I . . . am. In. Control!" My resolution was stubborn.

The deceit peeled off me like Spenz's mystic binding as I exited through to embrace the terrible healing heat. Oh, how the heat melted into me, cooking me as heat had never done before.

My heart raced and raced.

My renewed consciousness enveloped my deceit's shreds, casting them back into my being's cocoon.

The heat . . . the unbearable heat . . .

Oh, how I needed it.

I could not.

"I will not let you control me, my piece. If you control me, you control everyone in the Party who is connected to me through you."

I would not let this happen.

Swen would not let this happen.

Demonslayer would not let this happen.

We would not let this happen!

Kute. Ding. Juna. Gravelp. Thalla. Limbus. Steadfast. Patina.

No one would let this happen, and I would not fail them!

Chapter 22.1: Ygl's Charge: Aftermath

My eyes opened again. The bluish-yellow sparks—gone. Wisps of Swen's gases, all that remained.

I was suspended, Swen's curdling gases holding me high. Welbern weighed me down within my back scabbard.

I settled on the ground, feeling whole again, feeling strong.

I felt like . . . me.

Like me, but not like me. Would I be myself anymore again? With the evil that coursed through me like chilled lightning?

My genie coddled me; behind her cosmic eyelids, a lingering sadness cared.

"Swen." I sighed. *"I do not think I can do this anymore."*

So calm. How calm Swen was. *"Thou must. There can be little fuss,"* she soothed.

"I-I am so scared."

"I am too. We must see this through," she reassured.

I whimpered. A general. Now, a king. I never thought I would—not a moment like this. *"I . . . I do not think I can."*

Her curdling gases pulled away, exposing an apparent gash in her flickering dress, a gash uncovering whirling, starry masses accompanied by stagnant blinking vapors with bleeding colors—her cosmic innards? An eternity I dared not reach into for anything.

Her dress's gash shook a little. Her floating head drooped. *"It is up to thee. There's none I would love beside me."* Her eyelids blinked upward, intensifying her sadness. Her silvery mane swirled past me.

"Swen, that gash? How?" I asked.

"That need not concern thee. It is important to embrace thy dignity. Danger is on the way. I beg thee, here we must not stay." She trembled, trying to disregard her constant pain, the cosmic tear mending and reopening.

"Swen. It is me. Speak to me. Your hole," I commanded.

"Welbern should have killed me but spared me."

"Why you?"

"I'm of Man but not. A curse I've wrought. I tried protecting thee. Demonslayer sensed our singularity."

"Me?"

"Yes, in the cave. Thou I tried to save."

Swen. My mysterious Swen. She must have sensed the Death Mist attacking me but could not pinpoint where.

I pulled myself erect, still a little weary from the ordeal. The jodepiece buried itself deep into my right palm.

Brave Swen glided up and floated to my right, her nebulous gases acting as a caring barrier, her runes chiming.

My heart knew the lingering fear within me. My new merging felt different from the last. I knew that somehow I had changed into something different. I was not me, and this knowledge frightened me.

Ygl & the Dwarf

I could not defeat this Jode alone—this horrid Jode—but with Swen and Welbern, I thought I stood a chance, despite the absent Divinity.

Yet fear, for the first moment in all my life, gripped me like a manticora's thousand teeth. I almost dreaded taking another step, yet importance weighed heavy for me not to let anyone witness my discomfort. This was why I kept a telepathic sending with Swen.

Swen's riddle returned to me. *I must find the "sea of sand." I must find the "hidden green."*

An ocean of bewildered faces greeted me, an amazing array of Dwarves encircling, stretching out from the Grand Core's depth. Los and Num's sunlight tickled these ruddy faces. Expressions that raced with awe at witnessing Swen's greatness within their twenty-foot circle.

Yes. The battle had ended. Quirm fled. The Dwarven estate was saved.

Patina's unbridled interest pulled her closer. Her fashionable chain-mail tunic and armored vest were tarnished from the fight. "Nolly gee, what is this, King Eagle?" she asked, chewing on a bit of root.

"This, Princess Patina, is a genie. Swen is her name."

"She . . . she is a member of your Party?"

"Like Prince Kute, Queen Juna, and Ding. Yes."

The frazzled princess gasped. "N-now, that genie right there is of the legends? By Pariot's Hammer of Sacred Magma, how do I find myself saying this is impossible?"

"I am possible, Patina of the Dwarves. Believe the stories of the bards," Swen attested.

Patina gasped, grabbing a new root to chew on from her vest. "By Henc's Axe of Winter."

I understood my new ally's astonishment and the murmurs stirring, especially from the atheists.

"It is true. Believe them," someone snarled.

The crowd parted, exposing the rough growl I knew so well. Out of a crater smoldering from shattered blocks of ice, my favorite Dwarf climbed. However, he—she—no longer wore her familiar stained tunic and bunchy bearskin pants. No, a dead Dwarven warrior had provided her new metallic apparel, including a double harness sporting tomahawks. She did not model a long chain-mail skirt like some of the female rebels, maybe because her retrieved armor was from a male.

"Ding! I am so glad to see you!"

As Ding struggled out, a common helmet hugged her side, revealing an inverted, U-shaped anterior with a visor attachment.

As she trudged across the bloodied ground toward me, her paraphernalia missed a good pair of boots, like a Khunian Elf.

Ding examined me with a sneer and a grunt. "You made it. I did not think you would."

"What are you saying, Ding?" I asked. "You are the one who took my piece from me."

She said nothing, as usual, while stalking through the crowd. *"A minor price to pay when dealing with the greatest devil."*

Ding's telepathic sending shocked me. *"Ding, why? I am your friend."*

"I call no one my friend," she remarked.

"Whew, Ding. You drive such a hard bargain. But I am glad you are still here."

No response. I did not have to read her mind to see the pain in her eyes.

Ygl & the Dwarf

Ding turned to the crowd. "The Elf is right. As much as I hate to admit it, the gods are real, folks. I have seen one of them for even a brief moment— Ethnel, the god or goddess of the Faerie. I could not tell who Ethnel was. They called themselves the Essence of Preservation. I know it is hard to believe, but I have.

"I have even marveled at what I have experienced during my journey with this Elf. Xurchon's power is overwhelming, and as you have seen, this jewel, this piece of the Jode the Elf possesses, is not without its purpose.

"I beg you. Let us band together—all Epis, Mesos, and Endos—and resolve our differences for now. And believe, if even for this one moment, there truly is a Henc and Pariot, as much as it angers me to wonder where any of them are. If anything, be angry at their complacency. Be angry at their inaction."

Patina interrupted. "Please, Ding. Have faith—"

Ding looked her princess over. Not an ounce of anger flushed the thief's face. "Faith is a hard thing to hold on to when dealing with complacency. I am sure you understand, Patina.

"Why does believing in the Divinity have anything to do with establishing peace? Look at our kingdom. All this classism. Where were our gods while Mesos and Endos were being treated like trash by the Epis?"

"I agree with Princess Patina, Ding," I added. "I have encountered the Divinity more than once during our journey, and I have the same questions, but it is my faith in knowing something good might happen that will help us." My Achal, I sounded like such a hypocrite. "We all need each other to win no matter how agnostic we can become. Anyway, we have to stop this arguing. An entire continent is in trouble. We need all the help we can get."

No one responded. I disliked moments like this, only one person in control at this juncture.

"We will follow you wherever you go, Ding!" a Dwarf yelled.

Other Dwarves yelled praise with such respect.

Confounding. What did the Dwarven royalty do to their people? And apparently, I had lost the rest of my dialect. I could no longer call my people "k-k-kin." That was very hard to say.

Like an Ogrean statue, Patina said nothing, but her concerned features spoke volumes.

"This is your game, Ding," my sending stated. *"You wanted to be a leader. Welcome aboard. I only ask that you make your decision quick."*

I had never seen Ding look so uneasy. She appeared to search for someone or something throughout her adoring supporters' ruckus.

"I . . . I do not know," she answered.

"Well, you better know—and quickly," I suggested.

"I . . . I . . ." Ding struggled. The crowd simmered down, seeing their chosen leader ready to address them again. "We—"

"Do not worry. I am here," I encouraged her. "So are Swen and Patina."

My Dwarven friend still searched, her worry hidden behind a mask of strength.

I wanted to invade her psychic privacy.

"H-has . . . anyone seen Dong?" she asked her supporters.

Well, I guess I did not need to invade it.

Again, the building crowd fell silent.

"Who is Dong?" I asked Patina.

"Dong is the love of Ding's life," Patina answered reluctantly.

"Has anyone seen Dong?" Ding, impatient, asked again.

Patina would not catch my eye. "He is . . . her husband."

"Oh, Ding." My heart sank.

"No, we have not seen him," someone answered.

"Was he still in prison?" someone else asked.

Ding, failing to do a good job at seeming stoic, shared a look with Patina.

Still, my vexed friend struggled on. "Hey, the Quirmeans and their mist attacked all of us. At least, those of us in the Peri-world and some parts of the Epi-world. No one else had a chance to do much of anything during that horrible day."

No amount of stoicism could impede my friend's tears; Ding stood strong despite the pain, trembling slightly.

"Ding, I understand," I comforted. "I know. We all know. We have all lost. Wait, Swen?"

"Yes, master. What's the matter?" my genie asked.

"You can see everywhere?"

"I am all-seeing, though limited in distance. My Couch of Omniscience provides better assistance."

"We cannot wait for that. Are you able to see the prisons?"

"They are a little northwest of here, hidden in the hills," Patina advised.

"With my Couch of Omniscience, I can see the route," Swen stressed. "Yes, I can. What is thy plan?"

"Go find Dong and bring him here."

The runes on Swen's disembodied bodice chimed, causing the other runes in her mist to chime. She chanted, "Spinning gases, do my bidding. Show me where Dong is hidden." Her nebulous gases spun about her, concealing her in a mystic cocoon, expanding and contracting into an amorphous ball that swirled into her lamp. "And when he is found, to my master we are bound."

She vanished in a lingering perfume of apricots and maple.

I looked around for Qualt. "Can somebody tell me what happened here? Where is the Dwarven king?"

Patina grimaced. "My pops has been taken by the Quirmeans."

"Patina, I am sorry."

"There is much for many of us to feel sorry for," she replied.

"What happened?"

"As you took control over their general—Spenz, I think you called him—he lost control of his barrier, so we charged across against his army.

"Some riders and I raced to protect Ding. Nolly gee, a simple casting of my magma corona was enough to intimidate many Quirmeans. Thank Pariot, I did not need to cast it. I did not want to hurt any of my folk.

"Well, um, Man's soldiers are good. They are good fighters, and I am glad we outnumbered them, or else it would have been a different scenario, I think. Anyway, I see General Spenz fall to the ground and you going through frets, and I do not know what is going on.

"Your barrier suddenly falls, and my pops finally arrives with the laser cannon pointing at their general. We-we . . ." Patina swallowed. "We were not fast enough to stop Spenz. All he did was whistle. Whistle. That is all he did."

"And?"

"They disappeared. I am scared."

I gasped, alarmed. "Quirm will try to invade with the Death Mist."

Sugary dew's scent. A twinkling wisp of nebulous gases expanded, exposing Swen rising, hovering over the bubbling vapors. Her gases rolled apart, exposing what was buried within. I could not tell what or who the figure was.

"Dong?" Ding gasped in disbelief.

A frail figure lay among us like a curled chick with a lengthy pair of gray braids, awaiting death in an ebony nest. I guess I expected a healthier figure of a hefty Dwarf.

Ding raced to her vulnerable husband, nebulous wisps fluffing on her wake. "Dong? Dong!"

Ding kneeled next to her companion, who curled hidden beneath an unruly blanket of beard, so scared to touch him. "Dong . . ." Her voice, beckoning, a far stretch from the Ding I knew.

"Ding . . .?" he croaked. "I thought—"

"Shh," she comforted. "I escaped. I came back for you. For our folk."

My Elvin ears heard their mumbles best. Unfortunately, my errant telepathy may have assisted my eavesdropping.

The haggard Dong coughed, confused. "I do not understand . . . Man came . . . When did you leave, Ding? Took us . . . told us . . . to join . . . to follow . . . Xurchon." He coughed again. "I . . . with many . . ." He wheezed.

"Water!" Ding lamented to anyone who could hear.

"Swen," I commanded.

"But—" Swen tried to question me.

"Swen, now!" I retorted. My anger, ceaseless. Swen looked at me, startled and hurt. Others did as well, only adding to my embarrassment. "I am sorry. Please, Swen. Help her."

My genie's floating runes chimed a different tune with her chant. "From the hydroyids and their daughters, let there be a flask from the many waters."

Huh? What is a hydroyid?

I noticed one of Swen's runes again, looking like Dicen Squish's tattoo, which marked victims of demonsia, transforming them into the Dicen, but Swen's rune had a slash on it. I would question her about it, but not today.

A *slish-slosh, plish-plosh* emitted from Swen's swirling nebula. When her gases leveled beside the Dwarven couple, a large flask of water emerged—a flask made not of metal, shells, or stone but endless liquid streams swirling on themselves, composing a seemingly finished polish. The streams cascaded up from the base, ending as a waterfall on the flask's lip.

Ding grabbed the flask, gingerly feeding the nourishment to her husband. She held his frail head so tenderly.

Dong yelped in pain.

Ding's whimper became a cry.

Some of the water trickled from Dong's lips, making it hard to determine if most of the sustenance went to the intended region.

"Drink. Drink, my love," Ding insisted sweetly. "Look. Look." She nodded next to him, knowing he could not see. "I brought Gore," she lied;

the Quirmeans had confiscated her diamond-headed axe. "Remember Gore? You made him for me."

Dong ignored her and tried speaking again, with difficulty. Almost too much difficulty. "We defied Man . . . and paid dearly . . ."

"He-he . . . promised me." Ding's shoulders slouched with guilt.

"Who did?" Dong's parted lips presented moistened cracks.

Ding seemed like maybe she should be drinking some of that water herself.

Their whispering continued.

"Who did?" Dong demanded. "How did you escape?"

"I was able to . . ."

"Surrounded by so many Epi-Dwarves?" Dong's blanketing beard rustled; his wrinkly arm slid out from beneath him, an arm mangled with bite marks, almost impossible to discern, the palest of all.

"Wh-what is this?" Ding implored, noticing the protruding punctured veins.

Fatigued, Dong coughed; he seemed so close to death. "They . . . they fed me . . . to their monsters."

"No . . . no . . ."

"They tried to turn me . . . and they failed. They failed."

"No . . . no . . ."

Dong's wizened eyes examined his wife. "My love, my ch-charm . . . you could have not escaped on your own."

"I-I did."

"Do not lie to me," Dong's cracking voice croaked. "They turned you. They made you believe."

Never had I seen Ding at such a loss for words. "I . . . I am sorry."

"We are atheists. We believe in no gods." Dong's chapped lips found the strength to persist. "You. Chose. To believe. So they could help you."

"I-I am sorry." Ding's sad apology, weaker than Dong's arm.

"We. Are. God," Dong insisted, defying his end.

"We are," tearful Ding agreed. "We-we are. I love you. I love you."

Dong noticed something different in his savior's voice. "You. You sacrificed me."

"No. No," Ding denied.

"You-you sacrificed me; the Dwarves . . . to Man . . . to Quirm . . ."

"N-no . . ."

"Not even I would have done such a thing."

"I . . . I . . ."

No words.

Ding had no more words.

Just tears.

How many Dwarves heard Dong's admonishment? None of the surrounding faces showed any emotion. If any did hear the couple's exchange, how many would question Ding's leadership? Or would they remain blind followers? After all, Ding had already admitted to believing in divine existence, and if I understood Dong's exchange with her, she could not have escaped execution on her own.

How did you escape, Ding? Dong was right. You could not have escaped, being surrounded by so many.

Not even I could have. Well, maybe now I could, since I wielded the highest of Lorellian divine rights. But certainly against the jodepiece, my heightened psionics would have not been enough and

I would have fallen—just as Methelo, Rolando, and Sylvia did.

No, Ding. You made a pact. A pact with Rondo.

A shiver rattled along my spine. She even hid her betrayal from Kute. *The Party of the Jode followed you blindly, Ding, believing in your story.*

Your story, a lie. My—our—trust in you, misplaced.

How selfish of you.

And yet, I understood why she did it.

I knelt beside my sinful companion as she held her limp mate closer.

"I love you. I brought Gore. I could never leave without Gore." The lying Ding's apologetic whisper, a little louder. Her body shook with her testimony, brimming with a delirium undeniable.

I tried comforting her, touching her left shoulder. "I understand, Ding. You were there when I lost my Thalla."

"Please do not let him reach death!" Ding screamed for anyone who would listen. "Do not take him from me! Do not take him from us! Do not take him! Do not take him!"

Almost every other Dwarf sobbed with her, enraptured by her plea, leaving others shocked, with no emotion. The class did not matter: Epis. Mesos. Endos.

The legends never spoke of Dwarves being such an emotional lot. I always thought they were like brash Ding until now.

So much emotion. So many people cared about one couple.

Like my ride in the laser cannon, Ding's message proceeded rapidly, and the chanting began and grew, except now, the Dwarves chanted Dong's name with his mate's.

"Ding and Dong! Ding and Dong!" These two must have been heroes to the Endos and Mesos. The adulation was astounding.

"Do not take him from us!" Ding's screaming was barely audible through all the noise. "Do not take him! Do not take him! I am sorry! I am so sorry."

Princess Patina ran to her subject and knelt, embracing the Dwarven thief. Patina knew she was in a tight spot, being the only royalty to have mingled among her people, later siding with her dad on Ding's execution.

Ding raised her knotted head, looking at Patina with an unexpected softness I had never witnessed on her ruddy face. "Please, Princess."

Horrified, Patina gazed at Dong's mangled arm nestled in the briar of his lengthy braids. "There is . . . there is nothing I can do," Patina stammered.

Their rapport, different than I expected. More than a princess supporting her grieving subject.

Was Patina actually against Ding's execution?

"Swen. Is there anything you can do?" I asked.

Embarrassed, my genie's floating head tried hiding within her billows. "He is too close to death; the prerequisite cannot be met."

When sweet Swen spoke, the distressed crowd simmered.

"No . . . no." Ding sobbed.

"You are a genie." My anger rose with my desperation. "You-you can do anything."

Swen's buoyant runes shimmered, including the one resembling victims of demonsia. "There are limits to my power. Other forces greater tower."

Ygl & the Dwarf

"There must be something," Patina demanded.

My Dwarven friend could not contain herself. "Please, Swen."

Swen's gases curdled and crawled between and among us as she lowered herself. A detached hand felt Dong's crown delicately, examining him. "Dong, I must ask thee one thing. Does thou share the same feelings toward Ding?"

Dong tried tilting his head so that glazed eyes could see Swen. Ding held him closer for support.

Could the half-dead Dwarf distinguish what was occurring? My telepathy wanted to read his mind, but ethically, it was beyond inappropriate.

Dong just stared and stared. He had to have been amazed, gazing at Swen's cosmic visage. "More than the deepest of hates . . . and . . . the darkest of despairs," he croaked.

Touched by Dong's confession of his love for Ding, Swen furrowed her contoured brows. Her empathy, amazing; her glance at me made me forget my Thalla. Swen's mysterious contours, her flowing silvery hair, her beckoning eyelids.

"Ding." Swen did not deter from our rapport. "Does it matter how Dong appears as long as he's here?"

"No." Ding dared not look away. "No, it does not. I just want my husband back."

"It is too late to save Dong from the end. A new being I must mend. The moment is here. The event has come. Let us right what has been wronged."

With spindly legs, Swen's gases curdled and crawled around all aspects of Dong's frail form, a playful twinkling almost preceding every advance.

Like a waterfall, her building fumes fell on him, convulsing, hiding Dong within.

Startled, Ding held on to her husband. "What are you doing?"

"What is thee is thine," Swen's chant answered. "Let that which thee loves most be entwined."

Swen's cosmic billows kept convulsing; an indigo flash seemed to flare. The convulsions increased as the fumes receded to their origins.

Dong disappeared in their wake, replaced by a double-headed axe. The axe's head was composed of meshed diamonds, the body of twisted metal and toughest mahogany, ending at a handle wrapped in thick black leather.

Her axe, Gore, returned—but not the Gore we knew. At the polar ends of the menacing axe's staff, a tassel of braided gray sprouted. Dong's hair.

Ding gasped at her weapon's lengthier staff. "You-you combined Dong with Gore, as one?"

Modest Swen sidled around. "What thou loves most is now a gift to boast. Eternal till the end. Beyond the mend."

Ding cried, hugging her newfound weapon. She rose slowly. "Thank you, Swen. Thank you. I-I can sense my Dong in there. I can sense him. I shall name him Gore-Dong."

Swen's gases swept upward, whipping around Ding's newly named weapon. Dong must have been a Meso-Dwarf, a smith who created Gore for her to defy their government. He must have been a traitor as well. I could see how she cherished both. "From thy hands Gore-Dong shall never leave. Until thy end, past thy reprieve." An erratic indigo flare flashed.

"What do we do now?" Patina whimpered.

Ygl & the Dwarf

The awkward crowd stepped away. Patina faltered within the gap, blotches of liquid metal spreading all over her. A divine right granted to her only if someone was—

"Killed," Patina blurted.

Or had met the Divinity in another way.

"They killed him. My p-pops is dead." Patina could not move. "I . . . I am the q-queen now." She struggled to find her missing dialect through her tears.

She could not move. Silence fell on everyone. A liquid metal tear glistened on her cheek and rolled off her cherubic face. "What do we do now?" she asked.

"Patina." Gruff Ding tried to comfort her. The thief's new outfit made her appear more dignified, a symbol representing the Mesos and Endos. "Q-Queen, there is no other choice."

"Ding is correct, Patina," I concurred.

"Quirm is the true enemy. Not us," Ding added softly.

"Ding," the new queen remarked with similar softness, "we were never enemies."

"So what do we do?" Ding asked, acknowledging Patina's empathy.

Patina's liquid metal dried into her pores, returning her to her natural state. She turned to the crowd. "We avenge my pops's death, folks. Our kingdom's pillaging. That is what we do. Quirm and its emperor must pay!"

Ding touched Patina's shoulder. "And I stand beside you."

"Too much is at stake, Ding," I enjoined.

"I know, Elf—um—Ygl. I need your help. Queen Patina, may I see your horn?"

Patina obliged.

I hesitated. "Ding, I-I guess you need a platform to stand on since you are so short?"

"Yes. And you are not that much taller than me. I am five foot three to, what, your five foot seven?"

I hesitated, catching myself. "Yes. You need me to create it. I am sorry. I am too weary to use this artifact anymore."

"I am not talking about that, Elf!"

"Ding," Patina mediated. "He is a king. At least have that much respect."

I defended Ding's impatience. "It is all right, Patina. Ding and I have been through much. I understand her anxiety."

"We all should," Patina agreed.

I also understood her problem with authority.

"Ygl, I was not referring to your jodepiece," Ding clarified.

Eager Swen glided forward. "It is for me to help with thee?"

Patina whistled with a gesture to the sky, calling Twilight, her tole. "No. With all due respect to your genie and you, King Eagle, there is such a thing as Dwarven pride, nolly gee."

I snickered weakly. "Oh, how I know about that pride. And I know about your stubbornness." I smiled at Ding, who turned a different kind of red than I was used to.

Patina and some Dwarves laughed.

Wa-wa. Wa-wa.

The assembly dispersed, allowing Patina's tole to land.

"Lo, Twilight!" The Dwarven royal turned to the thief, taking off her armored vest. "Here, Ding. I want you to have this."

"But, Queen, this is yours." Ding stepped back.

"And I want you to have it. How does it fit?"

Feeling more awkward, Ding handed me Gore-Dong and put on the fancy vest. "It fits." Ding seemed a bit redder than usual.

"Good, because I want you to have the entire outfit."

"But-but, Patina—"

"There are no *buts*, nolly gee. If you are going to help lead our folk into battle—"

"Wait. Wait. I am not going to the Cories," Ding argued.

"You are not?"

"No. I need to go with King Ygl to Kyblore Island to finish what was started."

"Ding, I can go alone with Swen," I encouraged.

"No," Ding countered. "Swen needs to take my folk to the Cories . . . if-if you do not mind me asking."

I brightened. "Look at you, Ding. You are a leader."

"Always have been, Elf. Do not push it."

"Ding," Patina warned.

"Sorry."

Patina continued. "Now, King Eagle, do you agree?"

"Of course I do. I could not come up with a better plan."

"Then, Ding the Prodigy, I think we need to climb on board, address our folk, and change into my armor."

Prodigy? How unusual that Patina would name Ding after the Princess Prodigy I met in Swen's mist when we escaped the Ogrean estate. Could Ding be the Princess Prodigy?

Nah.

Twilight knelt, allowing Patina and Ding to board her feathery spine.

I moved away. "But what about you?"

"Me?" Patina coddled her hand, sweating liquid metal. "I can make my own. I wish I had a piece of root to chew on."

Ding reached into the vest and pulled one out, handing it to Patina. "Like this?"

Gracious Patina smiled. "Why, thank you, Ding."

Twilight jostled to flap mighty wings, prompting frazzled Ding to grab her unexpected friend.

A friend? My thief has a friend.

"Hold on," the newborn queen commanded gently.

"It is OK, Ding. You will be fine," my sending encouraged.

"That is easy for you to say!" Ding retorted.

Silvery-black wings stretched, flapping into the sky with the tole cavalry following. Their ascent stopped and leveled not too far away to escape my Elvin vision capturing a younger friend trying to help her older friend adjust to standing.

"Maybe this was not such a good idea." Ding gritted her teeth.

"You are doing fine, Ding. Patina, you have her?"

"Yeah, I do."

Even as Patina held her subject's hand, an emanating violet glow flowed atop Twilight's spine to cool Patina's steaming liquid metal that clutched the tole's abdomen, acting as a brace for Ding.

Ygl & the Dwarf

Patina handed Ding her horn. Ding held it firmly.

Patina winked. "And Ding, you have a story to tell me along the way."

Ding hesitated. She blared the horn, loud and clear. "There are those who know me and know me well. Those who do not will know me now."

Well, I would have been a little more diplomatic, I think.

Farther into the clearing clouds, a thunderous boom flashed. A monstrous fireball propelled toward us.

"Swen, follow me," I ordered.

We rose to meet our new challenge—without my jodepiece, if I could help it.

Dwarves, wolves, and toles scattered. A nervous Patina stayed with her passenger and a couple of Tole Riders. Liquid metal spluttered and splattered within her violet aura as she created a shield to encompass as much sky as she could.

The tole began to struggle from the added weight. The fireball increased in size with its descent.

"Nolly gee, it is so big." Patina's root fell out of her mouth.

"Just hold steady, Patina. I will attempt to slow the fireball down."

"Can you stop that?" Patina asked.

"I can with Swen's help, I think. Swen?"

My genie's dissociated right hand dashed ahead of her, with her gas tagging along, making it hard to distinguish an appendage.

I tried keeping up with my supernatural ally—a challenge worth having—but hesitated, focusing on the air in front of the flaming behemoth.

Before I could harden the air—and Swen could complete her chant—the fireball swerved to the right.

"It is heading for that mountain."

"That is not a mountain," Ding corrected, annoyed. "It is a volcano. Pariot's Trumpet."

"What is a volcano?" I asked.

No one answered, too engrossed in the fiery orb's new move. The orb soared faster than before toward Pariot's Trumpet, disappearing within.

Worry could not escape me. Too much death. We had to stop Xurchon from getting the Jode, or there would be more.

Once we found it . . . I did not know what to do.

Chapter 23: The Brigade

Quirm, the road to Skavir
Home of the Torture House
Night

Limbus crouched with a fellow brigadier upon a pine tree's lower branch, grateful their Khunian armor's murkiness aided in keeping them hidden. The sheer green fabric dangling as sleeves and from the groin aided in the camouflage. Limbus understood that the Sprites created this fabric from weed-weaving, a divine right.

He peeked through the numerous leaves that looked like a chaotic mess of tiny knives pointing in every direction.

The goal this evening: save the Lorellian slaves being taken to the Torture House.

He hoped he could see Ploone on the road's other side, but he couldn't. Ploone would've been better at his side, but Limbus knew Ploone could lead very well.

His Children's Brigade and he had been following the caravan's northern route since late afternoon. Limbus could hear that the Quirmean guards felt unhappy about the late delivery.

"Reprisals?" one guard grumbled. "Why weren't these rowdy Elves placed in detention camps to begin with?"

"Don't question our emperor," another countered. "He is loved by all."

"General Spenz will build another offense through Northern Lorel."

"Yeah, but will it be enough to withstand those devious female Khunians and their allies?"

"Were too many forces sent to deal with the Dwarves? Weren't those squashy things subdued?"

"Where's this Jode?"

"Quirm was doing just fine without it. Why bother looking for a needle in a haystack?"

Limbus could hear that Man still loved their crazy emperor. And would die for him because the royal family and he had brought so much prosperity to the land. But why ruin such joy looking for a mythical jewel? No one could possibly attack their powerful empire. Why not isolate from the rest of Zaendara?

Yet Quirmeans loved their emperor, almost hauntingly, to a fault.

And Xurchon as well.

This night, Limbus watched the quiet captives—many elderly; others, younger men; a few children—lying crumpled together in the rolling cage, a consummate defeat the guards were quite comfortable with despite the lengthy trip. The prisoners' minimal whimpering melted with night's poignant silence. Some knelt in meditation.

Meditation. A Lorellian pursuit so foreign to his family. Ploone liked meditating, but apparently, it didn't work well with him either.

Nus and Anul's twin moonlight aided the torches with much-needed luminance. The younger Lorellians sat awake in the uncomfortable dwelling, staring not at the road but the branches—especially his.

Ygl & the Dwarf

A guard became wary of the odd behavior, peering up to Limbus's branch to see what was so interesting about a bunch of brushwood.

Limbus almost peed in his titanium armor.

Please let the guard think maybe boredom has set in, or a curious squirrel ran by—or a monkey.

"Stay here," Limbus said to his brigadier as he leapt off, causing the branch to shake. Lorellians could never be as stealthy as a surreptitious Khunian.

"Oh, Interim," Limbus cursed, hoping the guard didn't notice as he positioned himself with creamy Snip behind the pine's trunk.

But the movement proved too sudden, forcing the peering guard to move his steed closer to the verdant canopy.

The guard gasped. Before he could yell, "Shields up," a series of swishing sounds filled the air from Ploone's side of the path, a series of thuds following—a few lifeless guards fell amongst the neighing mares and feeble prisoners' shouts.

His bestie must've seen the occurrence and signaled the offense. *Well done, Ploone!*

"We're under attack!" a rear guard warned.

Limbus rode Snip to the road's edge from behind a bush, a notched arrow ready to fly.

His dirty Elvin face encountered a mounted Quirmean. He gasped.

With no Ploone beside him, the "Little General" didn't know what to do with the menacing Quirmean approaching. He had practiced combat in Khun with his dad, but on this night, close combat was real and personal.

This. The moment for him to prove his mettle, to prove his Elfhood. All he had to do was let the arrow go, and the blessing would be granted to him.

221

Limbus would not.

"Let my people go," he commanded, swallowing his fear. Feline Snip yipped in assurance, his lengthy tongue flagellating the air.

Maybe it was the guard's audacious grunt. Maybe it was the fact Limbus's infravision caught the cool glint of the guard's shield moving against exposed flesh's reddish tinge. Maybe it was just plain nerves.

Whatever the reason, Limbus released his arrow in harmony with his Children's Brigade's onslaught. Before he knew it, his arrow slid beneath the guard's breastplate, through the chain mail.

The guard gasped his amazement, toppling from his mare. "You Elvin brat!"

Limbus installed another arrow through his throat.

Limbus gathered his breath and nerves. Combating another Elf like Ploone was one thing. Combating an actual enemy this close was another.

He had to make his dad proud, this "Little General."

Guards convened upon the scene. Some had already fallen from the brigade's assault. Limbus's plan proceeded well despite the hiccup.

A female brigadier leapt onto the roof's edge of one of the rolling prisons, shooting an arrow into another guard's sword arm.

From the evening's shadows, another guard emerged. The strange broadsword he brandished appeared to melt out of nightly air as if the Quirmean swung his arm at the unaware brigadier, the sword a deeper black than a shadow's umbra.

Though the nimble brigadier leapt aside, the uncanny blade made its mark upon her vulnerable leg. In pain, she lost her footing; one foot fell between two poles on the prison's roof.

Limbus reached for an arrow.

His infravision caught a thick blue line with a serpent's head and wings slithering—no, flying!—across the road from the underbrush, coiling around the guard's leg and proceeding beneath the Quirmean tunic.

A coatl? Here? Was Chieftain Rungna nearby?

A force beneath jolted Snip and Limbus, causing the yipping asegafian cat to thrust its master into the nearby underbrush, knocking his helmet off.

Limbus lost hold of his bow, his arrows scattering. He rolled out of the bushes and turned, facing his new adversary.

Another strange guard was upon Limbus with another shadowy sword. Not as big as the first but more imposing. While Limbus dodged solid strikes, his infravision couldn't help but notice crimson emanations popping from the Quirmean armor's crevices.

The imposing guard sniffed the air from inside his helmet. "Ah. An Elvin child of royal blood," he hissed. "How unexpected." A set of jagged teeth glistened in the twin moons' light. "And such a treat."

A Demon? Here? If the Death Mist was here, all surely would be lost! The mist housed the Demons who had conquered his home, the Forest of Lorel. *Oh no.*

Limbus grabbed some dirt, casting his prize into the Demon's face, trying to speed around the vile adversary.

A third Demon appeared. Thinner. Smaller.

"Some guards are Demons!" Limbus warned his brigadiers. "Aim for the most vulnerable parts. Teleport as fast as you can. 'Port as fast as you can!"

The thinner Demon hissed. "Royal blood."

"Limbus!" Ploone yelled. "L!"

Limbus barely dodged the shadow-blade, scampering into the woods as asegafians teleported their masters away.

He had to make his dad proud.

Embarrassed, Limbus knew he needed to return to the fight and help his other brigadiers. Thankfully, he could not spot any hint of the mist's milkiness.

He veered around, fidgeting for the dagger attached to his leglet.

The second Demon reappeared within night's umbra, acidic breath searing Limbus's nostrils, lashing out.

Ygl's son clipped his nose, retreating. The small Lorellian "general" kept dodging and dodging and dodging, his dagger much smaller than the shadowy blade.

Limbus smelt the acidic breath again, but to his left. He leapt to an elm upon his right as a new shadow-blade almost ripped into him—except that he'd jumped higher than he normally would have.

Extra nerves?

"You're a spritely one, little royal," the salivating Demon hissed.

Limbus bounced off the elm and flipped over the shadow-blade and the Demon's shoulder, slicing his dagger beneath the helmet, landing perfectly behind his opponent.

Ygl would have been proud.

"Seems like this is not your evening, Demon." The Lorellian general's son dug his dagger twice into the Demon's lower back, but as he did, he noticed an emanation, an extra burst of energy, from his palms. "This is for my mom!"

Crippled, the howling Demon dissipated into the shadows—or with the shadows? Were these new Demons?

Limbus dashed into the forest before the Demonic breath grew stronger, his little feet doing their best.

The bitter stench, more intense than ever, the air warmer.

A third Demon with no armor popped out of the umbra, maybe ten feet tall. With a piling punch, the Demon knocked the wind out of the little brigadier general, casting him aside.

The thinner Demon leapt out and over hurtling Limbus, impeding the rattled lad's new path.

In the middle of the Demon's leap, a small puff of blackness streaked from Limbus's hip nearest to where the Demon landed.

The ground did not feel as hard when Limbus landed—at least not as hard as it could have felt when he tumbled. He rolled around to a wide clearing, exposing his attackers.

Moonlight slivers flicked with every step of the unearthly duo's assured procession.

"I thought you struck him, Kampy," the huge one tooted with a heaviness Limbus felt. If not for the bulky creature's wide stance, the smaller one would have been hard to distinguish.

"I did. I did, Elico. The servant at Rondo's castle was a much quicker kill." The hesitant smaller one looked like a decrepit four-legged spider scampering toward definite prey. "I don't see you performing any better." Kampy's knees and elbows jutted like long swords. Approaching swords. Close. Too close.

A rapid galloping like a thousand horses approached. A half-horse creature veered around Elico and Kampy. Limbus knew this dark centaur was the second Demon, hastening the attack.

"Fools. His goddess has kissed him." The hideous centaur boomed his warning.

"Mersa," Kampy heckled. "How was the play?"

Before Limbus could breathe another breath, Mersa the Merciless was already upon him, fresh from kills at the Theatron in the city of Wyp.

The nervous teen threw his wheeling arms up as a last defense, trying to cast his dagger in mid-flail.

No. That was not his misplaced blade, for within Limbus's palms, a telekinetic energy rippled, erupting a series of psionic daggers from the surprised teen's flailing arms. The psionic knives pummeled the stunned Mersa back to the Demonic leader's entrance.

Kampy the Decrepit and Elico the Huge halted, witnessing their leader's blocked offense. No doubt. Power—awesome power—seeped from this little one.

Bewildered, Limbus took a moment to understand Mersa's warning. Achal had blessed him with cousin Rolando's divine right! The Lorellian general's son had become an instant prince amongst Elves. Prince Limbus of Lorel.

Limbus gasped. Wielding such rambunctious energy was certainly beyond his youthful comprehension.

Sarcastic Kampy cackled with glee. "Are you all right, Mersa?"

Mighty Mersa produced barely a pant. "It will take more than that to cower me, little prince." He glowered. Nus and Anul's persistent moonshine was a saving grace.

The princeling arose, trembling, trying to call upon his divine right.

Too. Much. Fear.

He had to make Ygl proud!

"We have all night." Elico the Huge's voice echoed from every umbra, making him all-consuming. "I killed a group of college students in a tunnel. You're nothing."

Limbus trembled more at his fruitless effort. He fumbled with his gold leglet, searching for his misplaced dagger, handed down to him through generations, hoping, like an idiot, that it would somehow reappear.

He pulled at the leglet Ygl had given him at the spring dance before Man's invasion, molded as a facsimile of a unipegon's wings. The leglet unlatched, revealing the relief of Steadfast, his dad's unipegon, galloping in the winds.

The leglet clicked in Limbus's grasp into a weapon. A boomerang!

The Lorellian prince cast his boomerang, hoping Ploone's more skillful hands were in play. The weapon flew through the Demonic encroachment without causing a scratch and returned to Limbus with no bloody prize—but with a burning sensation. He dropped it.

"Ow!"

The Demonic trio cackled with hisses.

"Come on, you f-filthy second-rate shades," Limbus challenged. "You cannot hurt me! I am a Lorellian prince. Achal stands by my side!"

The Demons emitted heavier cackling hisses.

"What is wrong? You have problems breathing?" Limbus challenged further. "Do not let that slow you down. I am ready."

Kampy scuttled toward Limbus, the shadow Demon melting into the dark ground.

Elico the Huge loomed larger than before, blending with the canopies.

Mersa's eight rapid legs came crashing down upon the princeling.

Limbus cupped his inflamed nostrils, stumbling back.

A small furry figure appeared to one side of Mersa the Merciless, with bulbous mauve eyes glistening.

The creature disappeared.

"Yip! Yip-yip!"

Mauve eyes popped on either side of Mersa, and a long tongue lashed upon the rampaging Demon, making Mersa screech from unexpected pain. The mauve eyes reappeared upon Mersa's hump, followed by biting, scratching, and yipping on the baffled Demon's neck and shoulders.

"Yip!"

"Snip." Limbus gasped. But how was his cat able to touch Mersa's intangible, fiery form? How was the asegafian able to cause pain? For that matter, how was Limbus able to cause pain? Maybe it was the telekinetic energy?

"We got this, Limbus!" Ploone assured him as he emerged with some of the Children's Brigade upon their yipping felines in a sea of mauve eyes and snapping tongues. "For Lorel!" righteous Ploone commanded.

Another rustling to Limbus's right.

Mersa and Elico hesitated, sniffing the air, drooling more.

Snip teleported between Limbus and Mersa the Merciless, hunching with a flagellating tongue.

The coatl Limbus had witnessed earlier swooped out of the canopies' cover, growing larger, matching Elico's size. Elico tried to swipe at the coatl but didn't count on the flying serpent's quickness and agility as it dove behind Elico and diagonally in front. Its feathered, scaly frame wrapped around Elico's lower half, making the hefty Demon fall to the left.

Snip leapt at Mersa. Mersa swiped the yelping feline away.

Anxious Limbus flailed his arms at eight-legged Mersa before Mersa could resume an attack.

Nothing happened.

Smiling, Mersa turned to the floundering princeling, dribbling fiery acid.

Limbus flailed his trembling arms. His fear hit a pinnacle point, sparking his telekinetic energy to cycle through, making a barrage of psionic knives emerge—hitting their mark!

With a cackling hiss, Mersa leapt into the air, vanishing into shadow.

Limbus glanced about.

He had to make his dad proud!

From the left umbra, cocky Mersa's head popped out, uttering, "Princeling."

The Lorellian prince was not quite sure what bowled him over first: Mersa's unexpected attack or the incendiary breath.

Elico the Huge struggled against the coatl. "Mersa . . . it is another . . . This creature attacked me by the road."

"Mersa?" The coatl's young voice. Female? "Oh, Interim, no."

The coatl's bluish image unwrapped from Elico, flapping above. The temperature around the winged serpent dropped drastically to an almost-unbearable freeze; the image's hue receded to a very deep blue as the coatl's scales and wings shed into a ten-foot floating mane.

A brightness glistened from this sub-cold transformation. A brightness that made the defiant Demonic trio uneasy.

Mersa the Merciless dashed to assist Elico the Huge, who was closest to the new beast, but it was too late for the fading Elico, who became a wisp, out of existence.

Screeching, Kampy the Decrepit struggled against the numerous asegafians' snapping tongues, trying to swipe at the teleporting colony, trying to escape.

Within the floating mane, a brighter coldness flashed from a quartet of large eyes, vanquishing the struggling Kampy.

"Limbus!" Startled, Ploone noticed the brightness. "L."

The last of the Demons, Mersa, glared, steering closer to the floating icy mane, shadowy claws elongated. Huge bat wings unfurled from his lats, keeping Mersa aloft. Acidic breath flamed.

Skinny arms popped out of the floating mane, with four-fingered hands rising in defense.

Infernal power emitted from Mersa's monstrous claws.

The floating creature shrieked. Yes, definitely a female's voice. A very human female.

Limbus cast more psi-daggers, striking Mersa the Merciless's posterior.

Mersa arched in pain. Yes, it had to be the telekinetic energy.

Ygl & the Dwarf

The floating mane's lower region parted, revealing cavernous, toothless jaws. A hairy garland at the jaw's upper lip flapped wildly, with bright, wintry air's continuous explosion striking the bewildered Mersa's anterior.

Mersa the Merciless gnashed and gnashed at the overpowering radiance shredding his darkness, his acidic flame becoming a puff.

Mersa fought to proceed.

An elongated claw disappeared.

An equine leg became froth.

Mersa was gone . . . along with the silence that created him.

The mane's icy maw closed. Trickling warmth returned with late spring's slight breeze.

The shaggy creature hovered near the grassy clearing's surface.

The rest of the Children's Brigade and some Lorellians emerged from the woods. A few clutched their shoulders, still shivering from the cold snap. Ploone approached the closest.

Limbus edged nearer to his new ally. "What are you?"

"Why, I'm like you, little prince," the floating mane answered. Its glowing slits oozed a certain coolness.

"Another Elf?"

"No." The creature giggled; its scrawny arms squeezed a shaggy midcenter. "Isn't psionic power an Elvin divine right? You don't control magic. Man does. I am Jonas. Princess Jonas. Of Quirm. My divine right permits me to transform into beasts. If you haven't noticed," she bragged.

Oh, this was who Chieftess Lojstania of the Sprites was talking about. "Are you OK?"

"Sure, I'm OK. I'm Quirmean. We can withstand anything."

"My mother held her sides like that every so often when she was in pain."

"Well, I'm not her! I told you, I'm Quirmean," she retorted.

"I'm sorry." Limbus, bothered, felt the need to defend himself. "Why are you yelling at me?"

The creature hesitated; something seemed older about her. "You're right, little prince. I shouldn't have yelled. Even though it is your fault my father has acted this way."

Some Elves gasped at her statement.

"How can you say that? You attacked Lorel. I was there. We were having a spring dance—"

"That was preemptive."

"I do not understand."

"Quirm attacked you before you could do the same."

"We were never going to do such a thing. I would have heard my dad talk about it."

Jonas paused. Her quartet of eyes scrutinized him.

Limbus continued. "If you feel that way, then why bother to come protect me and my people right now?" Limbus attempted to peer into the glowing slits in the hairy hideaway. He wished he'd attained Ygl's telepathy.

"Because what my father is doing is worse. He has brought an evil god into our lives and forsaken our gods. We've got to stop him, and I've gathered Quirmeans who agree. I won't say any gods' names to be safe."

"I support you too." Limbus stepped forward. "We do not care about Quirm. We just want to thrive in peace like anyone else."

"Is that a promise, little prince?"

"Limbus. My name is Limbus, Jonas. Of course it is. My dad is king now, and if I was king, that is how I would rule. What were those things anyways?"

"Raaligor. Shadow Demons."

"Limbus," Ploone interrupted, his face flushed. He grabbed Limbus, sizing up the floating creature. He searched Limbus's eyes. "L, are you OK?" he whispered.

"Y-yes," Limbus faltered, almost caught off guard.

Ploone took his helmet off, placing his sweaty forehead against Limbus's, his whisper a little louder from anxiety. "Do you remember what we talked about on the mountain? Do you know what I fear?"

"But you said you did not—" Limbus tried to restrain tears. A stifled hope broiled within him to hear his best friend say what he'd always wanted to hear during eleven years of friendship. Eleven years of playing with each other. Four years of combat training. Eleven years of just being there. For each other.

"You," Ploone whispered lightly, almost ashamed. "You. I am scared of you and everything you are. I do not know what would have happened if—"

Limbus lifted his best friend's face with both hands, wiping Ploone's tears with his thumbs. He pecked his fellow brigadier on the nose, planting longer, deeper pecks upon the lips. Tender pecks upon Ploone's cool, salty lips, as if nuzzling him like an asegafian cat. Kisses as sweet as Limbus could ever be.

At first, Ploone gazed at Limbus through widened eyes shimmering with gladdened tears. How could he resist such a blissful response? He returned sturdier, hungrier kisses only a strong protector could ever give.

Friends—best friends—made the best lovers.

The floating creature scoffed, disgusted.

Ploone glared at Jonas, a little offended. "Thank you for saving my best of bestest, but who are you?"

"I'm a princess, little Elfling—Princess Jonas—and shall be addressed as such."

"Jonas," Limbus interjected, "we will address you as such when you give us the respect we deserve."

Ploone added, "You don't look like any princess I would know or want to know—"

"Ploone." Limbus cautioned his newfound love, turning to Jonas as their asegafians approached with the surrounding crowd.

The Quirmean princess-turned-renegade noticed the gathering. "Well, Prince Limbus, we should all hurry and be on our way before my father's soldiers see what has happened."

"Where are we going?"

"Back to Rungna."

"You met Rungna-Olivia?"

"If that's her full name. Yes, I met her in Lorel. My followers and I helped her beat back my father's soldiers there. They didn't see what was coming before it was coming." Proud Jonas blew on three of her four nails. "Are we going?"

So this was why Chieftess Rungna had the children perform their reconnaissance of Chrot: to protect them from her challenging attack against Man's much larger forces. Rungna and her Khunian

Elves were never comfortable with children, being practicing celibates.

"Um, yeah. Sure. I just need my dagger and leglet. Ploone, can you have the others look for them?"

"We have to go," Jonas insisted.

Ploone and some brigadiers ran to fetch the dagger.

"Now, you wait, Jonas," Limbus asserted. "You need us like we need you. That dagger and leglet—especially the leglet—have been passed down in my family through many years."

Taken aback, Jonas smiled. "How old are you?"

"I am fourteen years old."

"Hmm. I'm nine years older."

"That does not matter. You're not better than I am."

"Boy, a little defensive, are we?" Jonas peered beside him. "What's that?"

Limbus looked down. A wagging Snip held the missing leglet in his mouth. Overjoyed, Limbus knelt down, hugging the faithful feline, pulling the leglet. "Oh, Snip, you're fine! You're fine. I knew that was you attacking that Raaligor." Happy Snip's long tongue wrapped the princeling's face, licking Limbus's nose. "Are you OK, boy? Are you OK?"

"Yip-yip."

"Well, you Elves are an emotional bunch, aren't you? So much for that vaunted meditation I've heard about," Jonas observed, amused. "You've got your leglet, at least. Let's go."

"Not until my brigade returns. I am not your slave." Limbus felt more confident. He noticed that the Quirmean princess was hurt. "I am . . . I'm sorry. I didn't mean that. I mean, I meant that, but . . ."

Ploone teleported in, smiling, seated upon Winky, dangling Limbus's dagger.

Relieved, Limbus continued. "Thanks, Ploone. Can you get everyone here as soon as possible? We need to leave."

"With that?" Ploone asked, alarmed.

Jonas's four eyes glowered through the shagginess, then gleamed. "You should be happy I'm in the form of a Northern Will-o-Wendiga. It keeps the Raaligor at bay."

"Whatever." Ploone ignored her, turning to his paramour. "We saved some Lorellians tonight, but some soldiers did get away, especially when winter started returning." He glanced at Jonas. "I can see what brought it."

"Ploone, she saved me from the Raaligor—"

"I know. I heard you yell, but yeah, I got Winky and the other asegafians, who gave one of them a good hurting. If I would have seen the one attacking you—"

"I know. I know." Limbus gave his love a reassuring smile. "I was able to too. I guess if they become solid enough, we can hurt them more. I have a divine right now, telekinesis."

"Cool. You're a prince now?" Ploone exclaimed, reflecting everyone's demeanor.

"'Cool?'" Limbus queried, smiling.

Ploone shook his head, ashamed. "Yeah, we're starting to sound more like Quirmeans each day."

"They were after you, princeling," Jonas stated.

"Me?" Limbus turned to his followers. "Ploone, can you get everyone else, please? We have to get out of here. I will tell you everything later."

Ygl & the Dwarf

"Sure, Limbus. You know I am here for you." Ploone kissed Limbus's forehead, then teleported upon Winky.

Limbus turned to Jonas. "Now, Princess—"

Before him presented half a Will-o-Wendiga with the upper body of a beautiful, steely woman in her early twenties, the floating mane hoisting her. Her skin was light, not albino like a Khunian Elf's. Her dark hair, kinky, not snowy.

She was not the princess in Limbus's memorial dream.

"Jonas?"

"Of course, Prince Limbus." She raised and wiggled very human fingers, her Will-o-Wendiga fur acting like a dress trailing from her forearms.

"I have seen Emperor Rondo. You don't have his hair."

"You have never seen my mother?"

"Not that I remember."

"Hmm . . . Seems everyone is being affected by memory loss. My mother is Queen Maxis. A Fumian."

Limbus gasped—that was the crowned assailant from his dream, the one who was chasing the snowy-haired princess and him down a cobblestone pathway in a marble castle's vast courtyard.

"Your eyes . . ."

"Yes, they seem Elvin, but all Rondo's children are a third Vantenian—from Vante, where they have slanted eyes. Hethomes was my grandmother. What would make you think we'd want to sleep with your kind?"

"What would make you think a kid would want to sleep with an adult?"

"Point taken."

237

"What were those Demons? And why me?"

"The Raaligor are among the elite of all Demons. You don't know about them? What do they teach you in Lorel? I thought you were historians." Jonas smirked, shaking her head in disapproval.

"Can you just tell me?"

"OK. As you can see, they are very powerful. They're not your normal class of Demon. They're members of the Truba, as elite as the Phorn, Sreggats, and Cindiru. They evolve from the blackest and most infernal of shadows. If Xurchon sent them, it's because he's at his wit's end. There's something happening in Zaendara. He's desperate."

"You're telling me. We have lost our dialects. Well, I'm glad you recognized the Raaligor."

"I did not."

"You didn't?"

"Not at first—until I heard Mersa's name. We're in trouble."

"But you killed them."

Jonas's face soured. "Killed? You think they're dead? They don't die, Lorellian. They're just vanquished back to wherever they came from until they reenergize."

"Oh."

"They'll return. Have no doubt about that. They will. The only thing that weakens them is harsh coldness and light. That's why I'm a Will-o-Wendiga. It's the only thing I could imagine, being a shape-shifter. Me staying in this form will protect all of us."

"But I hurt them. And the asegafians did too."

"You are of divine right. I can't explain the cats. As you know, my family's divine right is magic. We each control magic in specific ways while our father commands all our different scopes of power, except our mother's. I'm sure it's the same for you."

"Yes, Uncle Methelo controlled everyone's psychic powers."

"Yes. Psionics is your divine right. No one in my family has psychic powers. I see Rungna's divine right is speaking to animals, and her husband, Blasmle, creates minor storms."

"But wouldn't you be able to do that?"

Jonas proudly smiled. "Not me, but other family members' scope of magic is greater than mine. Uncle Spenz creates anything when he plays music. Uncle Werkle dances his magic into existence. That's what makes our divine right better than the rest. Even yours."

"Wow. You love to brag, don't you?"

"Well, we kind of are the superior race, but that's neither here nor there at this juncture."

"My bloodfather must be doing something good out there."

They looked at each other, shocked that a piece of Lorellian dialect had returned.

Jonas smirked. "I'm sure your 'dad,' General Ygl, is." Her mane rippled up her arms. "Now, let's get out of here. Your Rungna and Blasmle are waiting for us."

"We can't go until everyone's here."

A rustling in the trees made the duo jump into defensive positions. Snip wagged his tail.

A scattering of leaves trailed from the canopies, transforming into ethereal Sprites, at the head—

"Chieftess Lojstania. How did you find us?"

"You forget, Limbus. The leaves speak to me." Chartreuse wings carried her before him, concern clear upon her brown face. "Hurry."

"What's wrong?"

"I know you can't see it from here, but your family's Majestic Treehouse is in jeopardy."

My home! Mom helped build it. "How?"

"Man has set it ablaze. We must hurry to save what's left. We were fighting Man in another part of Lorel. We didn't think about saving it. It may be too late."

"I must go now." Limbus glanced at Jonas from his eyes' corner.

"Go, princeling." Jonas restored to her Will-o-Wendiga form. "I'll wait for your brigade."

EPILOGUE: Queen Squash

Bor, the Ogrean estate's capital
Late evening

Queen Squash slumped against her arid bedchamber's marble walls, sweat drizzling down her tired face as she held her swaddled girl close.

How long had it been since the Death Mist attacked her kingdom? Days? Weeks?

She could not tell. She remained focused on sealing the palace's windows from the invading mist with more marble. Ogrean windows were fashioned much like the rolling gate of her kingdom's monstrous wall.

When Squash latched her window's rolling shutters closed, she feared the mist might try to discover a way in, like through a gap. So with her divine right, she transformed the place where the panels closed into falling sand, which transmuted into a marble sealant.

Satisfied with that, she sent her messengers on kiradouras, and farther out on gryphons, to warn the populace to shut their windows. Not a small order, considering the nightly Dicen attacks, but the opportunity to warn her populace about the mist's significance was limited.

How many Ogres would abide by a long-term curfew to stay indoors? Oh, great Falvanch and her Club of Order, why did Smush not take Ygl's warning more seriously?

And she held her swaddled baby close.

With much of the populace warned, Squash focused her divine right beyond her palace at the surrounding homes' windows, sealing as many as possible. She shuddered, imagining the terrified residents of her kingdom's border towns closest to the wall. Her guilt impressed upon her the urgency of her actions.

Why could some Pixies not have stayed behind to help?

Her divine right reached as many households as possible, sealing windows and doors. Her bewildered residents would thank her when the moment arose.

The Ogrean queen knew not how long she kept at her task, but lives were at stake from this hideous mist.

She barely ate for days, too focused on maintaining her divine right, sealing everyone in.

And she held her swaddled baby close, not once looking down.

One day, she transmuted her marble window panels into quartz so that she could peek out, squinting from dawn's piercing hello. The mist curdled on the other side, pressing against her defense. She peered closer—three Demonic claws pawed at her.

She screamed, reversing the transmutation to marble, leaving a small dot to allow a pinpoint of light in to calm her growing insanity. And she held her swaddled baby closer, not once looking down, transfixed on the pinpoint.

She remained slumped against the wall for who knew how long, waiting and waiting. Each day, she would widen her quartz dot to see if the mist had finally left.

Ygl & the Dwarf

One late evening, it did. She returned the marble to its original state, opening the shutters, allowing cooler air in. And she held her swaddled baby girl closer, her tits sagging a little lower.

Queen Squash heaved a sigh of relief, knowing her eldest, brightest son, Crumb, remained on the battlefield, advising King Smush. Her stalwart middle son, Punok, guided their forces to a sure victory against treacherous Gravelp's allies.

But everything was confusing. How could the Party of the Jode be evil when their warning about the mist proved true?

Why did her daughter, Gravelp, kill Crumb's wife, Squish? What was the purpose? Why did Gravelp kill all those orphans?

Delirious Squash could not and would not understand her second-youngest child's antics, only happy to have a younger female to take her mantle.

Squash at last smiled down at her baby girl, swaddled in the soiled linen she could not bring herself to change, too busy thinking about her populace, the demanding duty weighing heaviest on her mind.

Squash gasped.

Her baby's unmoving eyes relayed enough. Her little girl and she had remained sealed so long, Squash had forgotten her baby's tiny lungs could not handle the limited air. The child had suffocated.

Perhaps. Perhaps Squash had held her baby too close? Perhaps she suffocated her own child.

Squash wept and wept and wept, her guilt weighing heavier than anything. She laid her unmoving infant in a porcelain cradle on a granite desk, wrapping her corpse in silks.

How many Ogres met end?

How many? How many Ogres died? Because of queenly foolishness. She had done the best she could.

She thought about returning to being a teacher, a much easier life.

Squash awoke, her head near her baby's cradle.

What had happened? She must have dozed in her despair. Maybe fainted.

A dream returned to her from her dozing. A memorial awakening reminding her of when, as queen, she had led a school of children on a field trip through the Ty's arid desert. She wanted to teach them about the animals. She made sure a wide awning shielded the entourage, hoisted at four corners by palace subjects. The Ogrean administration believed in serving their public to the utmost.

"Will Ty toad make meet end-of-shifts?" a curious student asked, not a mile away from her kingdom's craggy walls. "End-of-shift" meaning "death" in the Ogrean lost dialect.

"Well." Queen Squash hesitated, knowing the child's youth. She did not want to worry anyone. "Toad comes out cloudnoon, to hunt under moons. Have nothing worry about. Now, doggy caticus be fun, if find it."

"Why?"

"Doggy caticus not eat meat. They not even plant eaters."

"They not eat meat?" another child asked, kicking the ashen granules before a teacher admonished him.

"No. They lick sand and very playful."

"Why not pets?" another student asked, glancing at nearby bushes.

Ygl & the Dwarf

"Pets? In mountaindom?" Squash laughed. "They lick sand. Better stay out here where more sand before we lose mountaindom."

The students laughed along with their teachers. Squash missed this, teaching.

The ursine kiradouras' shells kept their riders cool in the twin suns' dry heat. The participants' delicate white apparel was an efficient supplement.

"What that over there?" a teacher asked, pointing to a lone rider descending from the cloudless firmament.

"I . . . I not know." Mystified, Squash peered closer through her draping hood at the plunging winged beast the visitor rode. The guards encircled the envoy, especially her.

The winged mare landed twenty feet from the gathering. Its bleached hide blended well with the rider's pale armor. As white as white could be, this pairing.

Except for one item: the rider, though as big as an Ogre, had a much lighter complexion and a thinner frame. She could not see his face, shaded by a wide, floppy hat he donned when he slid off his mount.

"That not Ogre or sphinx," she realized.

When the visitor approached, their eyes met. His, the kindest she had ever beheld, with a face slightly younger than that of her husband, King Smush. The wisps of gray on his temples did not escape her.

"Who you?" She fidgeted. Her guards closed ranks more tightly around her; their kiradouras growled softly, their weapons at the ready.

"Please. I am Alduur of the Giants." He beckoned. "I must speak to your leader. I have a most dire message of highest priority."

The adventure continues.
Catch up with the adventure, starting with
Part One: *General Ygl and the Genie*

PJSelarom.com

About the Author

PJ Selarom, an air force veteran, is a lover of mythologies, inclusivity, and comics. He ventures to combine these ideals in his wonderfully dark adventure of love, religion, and politics.

He resides in a treehouse somewhere in the country, taking care of his baby unipegon.

He can be reached at
PJSelarom.com/contact.